Gutter Punch

A.J. Stanton

URBAN PIGS PRESS

urbanpigspress.co.uk

ISBN: 9781068626166

"People will believe any old shit"
- Immanuel Kant, 1804

Chapter One

Sam Carter felt around his lower regions and began playing with his semi-erect penis, although a few moments of this and it was abandoned with the full knowledge it would prove a fruitless task. He could taste a mixture of vomit and cheap whiskey on his teeth and his stomach wasn't particularly impressed by either. He did believe, however, that there was just as much chance of him messing himself as there was of him being sick and was frightened by the prospect of both. He eyed beside his bed a glass of water and drank thankfully.

Sam made a slow, zombie-like dawdle to the bathroom and then, feeling slightly better, made his way to the lounge. Curled up on the sofa with a suit jacket draped over him was a pale looking young lawyer by the name of Ford.

Sam squatted on Ford's legs in a successful bid to get him to sit up. He fumbled around under the sofa, eventually finding a crushed packet of cigarettes. Sam lit one up and took a long drag.

'What are you doing here?' Sam said, a puzzled look on his face.

'You don't remember?' Ford replied, rubbing the sleep out of his eyes. 'I had just finished a long case. A couple of us decided to go for a quick drink in the bar around the corner from the court. Didn't expect to see you in there. You were a mess, kept saying you were celebrating something and trying to force alcohol into me. I ended up having to take you home before you embarrassed me any further.'

'I was celebrating,' Sam said, letting out a cloud of acrid smoke. 'I got fired yesterday.'

\#

As soon as Sam had started at the newsroom, he found it deeply unrewarding. His work life consisted mostly of following leads and compiling reports of all the unbearably dull stories no one else wanted to touch. If the news programme was going to be short a few minutes, then it was Sam's job to sift through the local papers for some sort of fluff. Human interest stories, whatever that meant, the most recent one having been about Mr. and Mrs. Gordon's cat, Sebastian, which curled up and went to sleep in the laundry basket, only to end up getting stuffed into the washing machine and whacked on spin cycle, and still somehow managing to survive. Sam had to interview the family and get some good footage of the cat. He had done several of these stories. Cats plastered into walls, trapped under floorboards, set in concrete, and miraculously they all seemed to survive. A cat lasting three quarters of an hour in a washing machine mixed up with detergents and semi-boiling water seemed unlikely. Sam had quickly pieced together in his mind the real series of events. Mrs. Gordon, on finding the saturated corpse of her daughter's cat had held down a deathly scream. She showed it to her husband, holding it at arm's length despite the fact it was quite clean. Mr. Gordon had immediately rushed out to the nearest animal shelter for a replacement, stopping on the way to throw the dead one out the window and into a ditch. Sam had considered exposing this fraud. It would simply take some last-minute changes before airtime. But he didn't. What would be the point? It wouldn't achieve anything, except for upsetting an eight-year-old girl and possibly some cats. Instead, he had half-heartedly noted down the story while the Gordons, eager to be appearing on television, helpfully dunked Sebastian Mark II in the kitchen sink and then stuffed the startled looking kitty into the laundry basket. A dramatic reconstruction.

Sam was almost relieved yesterday afternoon when the boss had called him into his office. Sexfiend for all intents and purposes was the man's name. He was a short, fat, balding bastard with a dynamic personality. Sam had stood there in Sexfiend's luxurious office, wincing at the ferocity of the glower he was being subjected to.

'Do you think I am stupid?' Sexfiend asked, almost as if he wanted an answer.

'No sir,' Sam said, trying to sound sincere.

'Shut the fuck up,' Sexfiend roared. 'You may have gotten away with it for a long time, but no more. No fucking more you worthless piece of fucking shit.'

Sam knew exactly why Sexfiend was angry. He had expected to be "let go" a long while back but he had never been discovered. For about the last year, tiring of following stories and reporting what actually happened, Sam had begun just making things up. It had started quite small. Events minor celebrities supposedly attended. It later moved to made up politicians of non-existent countries dying in all manner of ways. Floods, executions, bear attacks and sometimes even natural causes.

'I could have you killed,' Sexfiend stated with a smile growing across his chubby face. 'I should have you killed. God knows I'd like to. But instead, I am going to be kind. Clear your fucking desk and get out. But watch your back pal. I could have you killed so fast, you wouldn't even know you were being killed.'

#

'So, you really got fired?' Ford said. 'I knew you would, sooner or later. You were always turning up drunk because you've been hanging about with Sea-mouse too much. Your problem is you never take anything seriously'.

Sam began to switch off at this point. When Ford got going, he could berate people for hours. It was one of his character flaws.

Sam and Ford had been flatmates whilst they were at university. Ford was a conscientious law student that no one apart from Sam could tolerate. Sam on the other hand, spent his years at university in a drunken paradise. Occasionally mooching into lectures between bouts of heavy and sustained drinking with his oldest friend Sea-mouse. As soon as Ford had met Sea-mouse he had disapproved of the man. He stood for everything Ford disapproved of, and that in Ford's mind was grounds for disapproval.

'What are you going to do about work?' Ford asked. 'You ought to go job hunting as soon as possible.'

'I don't know,' Sam answered. 'I might take a couple of days off to rest before I start looking. I have a couple of contacts in the papers. I did a little bit of freelance for them. They're only tabloids but I reckon I could get a job with one of them no problem. Or failing that, I think a couple of the investigators we've used in the past are hiring.'

Ford could barely believe his ears. How someone could take such a blasé attitude to a situation like this was beyond him.

'Actually, thinking about it, I might leave it a couple of weeks.'

Chapter Two

'I don't care if it will cost that much,' Vince yelled down the phone. 'Those scenes are going to be re-shot and you're going to fucking like it.' Vince slammed down the receiver and was almost immediately a different, calmer person.

Gloria, Vince's secretary, walked into the plush office which resembled something a seventies nightclub manager would not look out of place in. She was carrying a tray with a large cup of black coffee and the day's papers. 'You should have a look at page seven of this one,' Gloria said with a smirk as she handed Vince his morning pick-me-up and a copy of a particularly sordid tabloid. Vince grabbed them both whilst thumbing through his diary and she retreated from the style extravaganza that was his office.

Vince was obsessed with the daily papers since he had won that Oscar, the tabloids had made his victimisation their sole purpose, in Vince's mind anyway. Every time he was seen with a new girl, the next morning's headline would be, 'Superstar actor grabs himself another pair of golden globes', or, 'Love rat Vince cheats again.' Almost every aspect of his life was under the microscope. Showbiz columns were filled with his drug and booze fuelled shenanigans. Gossip about him being gay, gossip about him being bisexual, gossip about him being a sex crazed, womanising misogynist bastard. Around 90% of it was made up, and that didn't bother him. He could cope with that. It was the other 10% which was true that did the damage.

The story Gloria had directed Vince's attention to was particularly annoying. Leela Van Tsar, the woman he had been dating for the last month or so, an actress with her own series of teen horror movies despite being twenty-eight, had her face superimposed onto the naked body of a different young lady. All this under the slogan 'Vince's girl in the buff' with '100% fake' in small writing at the bottom. It hadn't even been done well, it was clearly a fake.

'She isn't going to like this,' Vince muttered. He glanced at the picture again. The model that had donated the body was in fantastic shape. He looked over at his en suite and then back at the picture. There was a stirring in his loins and he took the paper into the bathroom. Vince sat down on his designer toilet with the picture sprawled over his lap and began to go through the motions practised many thousands of times before. In a flash of paranoia, he wondered if the paparazzi had hidden cameras in his toilet, how embarrassing if this appeared in tomorrow's papers. It didn't deter him though and he continued what he was doing. He finished swiftly and efficiently, his seed splattering onto Leela's face with a most satisfying noise, and there was only a slight feeling of guilt running through his mind as he washed his hands.

He stared once again at the newspaper for a few moments, imagining what he would say to the editor if he were standing in his office right now. This was the man who had been responsible for some of the more sordid probes into Vince's private life. Rummaging through his bins. Tapping his phones. Paying prostitutes to pick him up in hotel bars and then writing articles about it.

The editor in question was David Morgan OBE. A podgy man with a thinning floppy quiff of hair that did little to cover his shiny, sweaty forehead. At that very moment, David Morgan OBE was in his own office, imagining what he should say to the man sat before him. A deadbeat, a bum. In fact, David Morgan OBE could not think of an occasion where he had come across someone such an instant disliking to had been forged so quickly.

'This isn't the first time we have met,' Sam said. 'I did a little freelance work for you. That article about the bank robbery last September. Remember, you met me then. You told me to get out of your way that time. You disliked me then, I think.'

'Aaah,' David Morgan OBE gasped enthusiastically. He had real grounds for contempt now. 'Don't take this the wrong way, but I don't like your work and I don't like you. I think that the best thing you could do now, would be to commit hara-kiri.' David Morgan OBE paused to consider this for a moment, 'In fact, on reflection, I demand that you commit hara-kiri.'

David Morgan OBE picked up Sam's CV as if it was a turd. He screwed it up and then threw it at Sam with a good, hearty throw. 'Now get out of my office,' he said as the paper missile bounced lightly off his target's forehead.

Sam, who had been sat through this outburst with a bemused grin on his face, got up and left the office. A journalist tapping away on an article briefly noticed Sam and gave him a sympathetic look.

'What's hara-kiri?' Sam asked.

'That's ritual Japanese suicide. Samurai who had failed their master in some way would mortally stab themselves to regain some honour before they died. He's always trying to get people to commit hara-kiri. He's told me to do it twice today already. He always seems so keen, I hate disappointing him.' The journalist looked around, then back at Sam. 'A young work experience lad actually did it last year,' he whispered. 'Poor lad. There was blood everywhere, the new photocopier was nearly ruined.'

With that, Sam left. It wasn't the worst job interview Sam had ever had, but he couldn't help noticing that it had gone badly. Sam's worst job interview was some time ago now. He had applied for a role with a large PR firm. He remembered being nervous, but Ford had briefed him fully the night before on the kind of questions he might be asked, all the right answers he should give, and he'd made Sam practice his handshake about a dozen times before he was finally satisfied it was firm but submissive enough. The big day had come, and Sam looked sharp in the suit Ford had lent him. He rearranged his tie before stepping into the office for his first big interview, all the questions he was planning on asking to make him seem keen rushing backwards and forwards through his head. What happened after Sam had opened the office door and stepped inside came as a complete shock, like waking up in the middle of the night to find yourself being wanked off by a ghost. He had come expecting a few questions about his education and what, if anything he knew about the company and the exciting world of public relations. Instead, Sam had been met by four middle-aged businessmen, their jackets off, sleeves rolled up, flinging chair after chair at him. They had dozens of them. That cheap plastic kind you used to get in schools, each man with his own, rapidly decreasing stack. Sam had been stunned. He just stood there, completely flabbergasted as chairs ricocheted off various parts of his body until eventually he was caught right on the chin. When Sam finally came to, he was told that it was a new interviewing technique a Human Resources consultant had taught them. Apparently, it was designed to gauge the candidate's performance under pressure. Sam was handed a moist towelette and told that he didn't have what it takes before quite literally being thrown out of the door.

Sam had three more interviews that day but to be honest, he couldn't be arsed. He made his way home, pondering his next move. 'Booze, that's what I need,' he thought.

#

Sam stepped into the 'Hare and Hounds', which was only a short walk from his flat. The old Tudor building had a certain romance about it; he could imagine Henry VIII doing one of his wives up the arse in the toilets. There was just that kind of feel to the place.

As anticipated, Sea-mouse was sat reading the local paper and swigging at a pint of Pernod.

Sea-mouse was quite a large man. He was large in a very non-threatening way. In the same way a grizzly bear would be non-threatening if it were made from fluffy, fireproof fabric stuffed with beans. Sea-mouse was also an alcoholic. He came from a long line of alcoholics. His father was an alcoholic, his grandfather was an alcoholic and so was his great grandfather. Alcoholism in Sea-mouse's family had been traced back through court and church records to the time of William the Conqueror. There is a gene known in mice that if possessed, then that mouse given the choice will choose alcohol over water and will drink itself to death. It is believed by many an academic that Sea-mouse and his ancestors all exhibited the human form of this alcoholism gene. In fact, Sea-mouse's family had been alcoholics for so long that an interesting form of natural selection had taken place. Sea-mouse's liver was now so advanced, so much more evolved than the average human liver, that he was almost immune to the effects of not only alcohol, but most toxic substances. To get drunk, Sea-mouse would have to drink at almost every waking moment, and getting drunk was a challenge Sea-mouse accepted each and every day.

Sea-mouse's face lit up when he saw Sam and he shot over to give him a big hug. 'I'm so glad you came here tonight. I've had a terrible bereavement in the family.'

'Your dad hasn't died again, has he?' Sam responded, a hint of scepticism in his voice.

'Yes, but this time I think it's for real. Someone who knows someone he drinks with sometimes saw him smash his car into a burning factory, come crashing out the other side and into a lake.'

This didn't sound very plausible to Sam. 'Have they found his body?'

'No.'

'Have they found any body?'

'No.'

The dubious look of concern across Sam's face disappeared. 'The next time I see Clive, I am going to punch him in the face.'

'You can't speak ill of the dead like that.'

Sam groaned. For as long as Sam had known Sea-mouse, which was some time, Sea-mouse's father had gone through short periods of being alive, closely followed by short periods of being dead. Sea-mouse's father managed to get himself killed at least twice a year without fail. Sam had once asked Sea-mouse's father why he kept faking his own death in the most unusual of circumstances. The strange man had stood there for a good half an hour, sipping at a bottle of brandy. 'I guess I just want that air of suspicion when I really do die,' he finally answered. 'It is the only way I can live forever.' Sam made no more enquiries after that, although he did keep imploring Sea-mouse not to believe it the next time his father passed away quickly during the night.

Sam knocked back a few beers and soon a warm, fuzzy feeling washed through his body. He began to hanker after something stronger and started on his favourite whisky. He talked and Sea-mouse listened and both drank until their conversations became incomprehensible to anyone but themselves. Sam forgot all about his recent employment problems. Nothing mattered and everything was perfect.

As the evening wore on, Sam found himself coming to the conclusion that he should phone his ex-girlfriend, Jane. They had lived together for nearly a year and for a while, things had worked out. Sam could never hold on to a girlfriend though. He just kept his cards too close to his chest.

'You keep your cards too close to your chest!' Jane had said when her mind was finally made up to leave.

Ring… 'Hello?'

'It's me,' Sam said, slurring so much that the words practically melted into one.

'You're drunk.' She sounded cross, although Sam did not pick up on this. 'What do you want?'

'I've been thinking about you,' Sam stammered. 'Perhaps I could come around, we could talk.'

'Not in that state you won't,' she snapped, 'goodnight,' and with that she hung up.

Chapter Three

Sam was sat on his sofa watching cartoons and eating chocolate ice cream. He loved to eat chocolate ice cream when he had a hangover, it settled his stomach. He had been asleep most of the day and it had gotten dark outside. He was supposed to be going to see Jane in about half an hour and was probably going to be late. She had phoned earlier asking if he would come round. Sam had expected her to be angry about last night, but she didn't mention it. She seemed more interested in explaining, in some detail, how she would like to sit on his face. The idea of this was getting him hard.

The doorbell rang; it was Sam's taxi. He quickly finished the ice cream and dumped the bowl on the floor.

'Alright mate. You call for a sherbert dab?' the taxi driver said in what seemed to Sam to be a fake cockney accent. Sam nodded and got into the beat-up old black cab.

'Archer Street please.'

The taxi rolled off and Sam hoped the driver would not try and instigate conversation.

'You watch the foootball last night? Fuckin' disgustin' wonnit!'

#

The taxi pulled up at Jane's house and he knocked, making a token effort at rearranging his erection so it was less noticeable.

Jane had a revealing low-cut top on and a tight pair of jeans, both of which seemed to be working in symbiosis to expose her toned midriff. Sam had to concentrate to maintain the status quo in his shorts; it was like being thirteen again.

'Sit yourself down,' she said as they wandered into the lounge. Sam had to remove three cushions before he was able to sit at a comfortable incline, one that didn't necessitate gripping the armrests to stay aboard the sofa.

'Here, have some wine,' she said, handing Sam a glass.

'I'm glad you called yesterday,' Jane said as she poured more wine, 'it's a pity you were in such a state, I would have liked to see you. I've been thinking about you quite a bit recently.' Jane took a sip and sat down closer to Sam.

'You look good today,' Sam said awkwardly.

'Thanks, you don't look so bad yourself considering what a mess you must have been in last night.'

She was very close now and Sam moved in to kiss her. Jane reciprocated and was soon lying on the sofa with Sam on top, fondling away. Sam didn't know if it was all the wine, but the room suddenly seemed to get a lot brighter. He hoped he wasn't going to pass out.

Gutter Punch

Jane had been struggling to get out of her jeans and Sam was in the process of pulling his shirt up over his head. Sam began kissing her again. 'It's really bright in here,' Sam said. 'Shall we turn the lights down?'

'No,' Jane said firmly. She reached her hand into Sam's trousers and started to rub him. Sam began pulling his trousers off when, out of the corner of his eye, he noticed a dumpy old man pointing a camera towards him. Sam screamed as he looked around. Sure enough, there really was a cameraman standing there, filming him. Not only that, there was a whole film crew. Lighting, sound, even a director. Sam screamed again.

'What's wrong?' Jane asked.

'There's a film crew in here,' he yelled. 'We're being filmed.'

'I had hoped that you wouldn't notice,' she said sounding slightly irritated.

Sam was beside himself. 'There's a whole bloody film crew in here.'

The director was pointing excitedly and the cameraman moved in for a close up of Jane's breasts.

'Yes,' Jane said, waving for the cameraman to back off. 'It's part of my new business venture.'

'What new business venture?' Sam was confused.

'I'm going into the porn industry. I'm going to make porn films and then sell them mail order, and on my new website.'

23

Sam was shocked to say the least,

'Just ignore them,' Jane said, pinching Sam's nipple.

'Ignore them?'

'Yes, ignore them. It'll be fun. Just like old times.'

'I can't carry on, it's kind of spoilt the mood.' Sam pulled his shirt back on. He pushed past the film crew and stormed out the front door.

Chapter Four

Gloria poked her head into Vince's office. 'The gentlemen from the detective agency are here.'

'Excellent, send them in,' Vince said. He was in a good mood today. An idea had formulated in his mind the previous night and he was taking the first step in retribution against those vile newspapers.

A large, powerful looking man strode into Vince's office closely followed by another, smaller man. Vince stood up, offering his hand, which the large gentleman shook with such vigour that Vince's eyes began to water.

'The name's Tony, and this is my associate Johnny Cheung.'

'Pleased to meet you,' Vince said with a grimace, retrieving his hand from Tony. 'Do sit down.'

'So, what seems to be the problem?' Tony asked. 'Some cunt blackmailing you, is it?'

'Um… no nothing like that.'

'You've been arrested and you want some cunt to get at the evidence?'

'Um… No.'

'Some cunt you've been fucking has run off with your fucking cash and you want the cunt tracked down?'

'No.' Vince was starting to get irritated, but he didn't let it show. Tony was a very imposing character.

Tony had run out of ideas and there was a look of deep thought on his face.

'Perhaps it would be best if you let me explain,' he offered. 'Have you ever heard of David Morgan OBE?'

'No, I haven't. Cunt, is he?'

'Yes.'

'So, what would you like us to do?'

Vince explained his plan. It was simple really. He wanted those journalist bastards to go through some of what he had to put up with every single day. He would focus on all the main tabloids, but especially David Morgan OBE's. If someone at one of these papers was cheating on their partner, Vince wanted to know. If one of them took drugs, Vince wanted to know. If any one of these fuckers was doing something they shouldn't, Vince wanted to know about it. He was going to make sure that all their dirty little secrets were known, and then he was going to spill the beans to their loved ones. He wanted to ruin their lives. Then there was Vince's pièce de résistance. David Morgan OBE would be getting a little something extra.

When Vince had finished, Tony sat in silence for a while. Johnny Cheung whispered something in his ear and Tony nodded. 'This is a big job,' he finally said as Vince looked at them both expectantly. 'This cunt ain't gunna come cheap.' Tony took out a pad of paper and a pen from his jacket pocket, wrote down a figure and handed it to Vince. 'This is what it'll be per hour,' he said.

Vince looked at the number and replied straight away, 'Fine, money is no object.'

'And expenses?' Tony added.

'Not a problem.'

'You got yourself a cunting deal.' Tony stood up and presented his hand so they could shake once more. Vince wanted to reel from this gesture but thought better of it. Tony was a very big guy.

'We'll get to work on this cunt straight away and report back to you each cunting week,' Tony said as he and Johnny Cheung left.

'Excellent,' Vince said, feeling as if real progress had been made.

Tony and Johnny Cheung walked back to their black Mercedes with big smiles on their faces. 'That cunt is a real whack job,' Tony chuckled.

'What an idiot,' Johnny Cheung said.

'Hey, I've got a cunting great idea. You remember that cunt who phoned last week?'

#

That night Vince lay awake in bed. He couldn't think of anything but the look on those little shits faces when they discovered what he was up to. Leela lay asleep next to him, but Vince didn't feel like sleeping. He poked his cock out of the opening in his boxer shorts and began to masturbate aggressively, and for some sick reason, thought of David Morgan OBE.

Chapter Five

As Sam walked down the street, he had to struggle to stop himself from scratching his behind. He had been in a rush to get out the door this morning, but he was sure he'd cleaned his arse properly. He had wiped until the paper was coming back clear, but somehow, some way, some shit had crept back onto his anus. It made itself apparent only a few moments after leaving the flat. Sam then had to endure a twenty-minute bus journey with the agony of needing to constantly scratch, really get his hand up there and have a good dig around. It hadn't helped that the bus was old and the aged vinyl seats had caused sweat to accumulate around his crotch. Now, as Sam walked down the street on his way to the interview, he was in a lot of discomfort. He considered finding a café or somewhere with toilets so he could clean himself up, but then he would be late. Stopping to wipe shit was a time expenditure Sam could hardly afford.

\#

Tony's HQ was situated in a classic sandstone building. It looked like any other office that you would expect to find in a nice professional area. If it wasn't for the sign, which read "Tony Maloney's Private Investigators: Surveillance Specialists", Sam could have mistaken it for a law or accountancy firm.

Sam stood outside for a while smoking a cigarette, gathering up the courage to go inside. For someone who didn't really want to work, Sam always found it strange that he would get so nervous before an interview. He stubbed out his cigarette, gave himself one last scratch and then went in.

The office was small and closed in. Or it was reasonable in size but just full of clutter. There were two large desks, both piled with files and papers. Grey, official looking cabinets were placed around the room, interspersed with the occasional rubber plant.

'Hello,' Johnny Cheung said. 'Please sit down.'

Sam did as the man instructed.

'You here for the interview?'

'Yes, yes I am,' Sam answered. He was getting even more nervous and began playing with the keys in his jacket pocket.

'Tony will be here any minute,' Johnny Cheung said sensing Sam's anxiety. 'Then we can get the interview under way.'

Sam's eyes began to wander around the room. To the left of him on the wall was a company calendar from some surveillance technology manufacturer. The picture for this month was a P4 micro camera. Top of the line apparently. To the right of him was one of those really annoying posters promoting teamwork. This one had a picture of a big oak tree and underneath it read, "Working Together Creates Strength."

It wasn't long before the office door flew open. A large man Sam presumed to be Tony waltzed in with the swagger of a tough guy. In his left hand, he carried an expensive looking leather briefcase. By the way he held it, it appeared light. Too light to contain anything. Sam believed it to be empty.

Johnny Cheung seemed quite excited. He always enjoyed seeing Tony at work, there was something unpredictable about the man which Johnny Cheung just loved. He was also slightly relieved that he no longer had to contend with this bum by himself.

Tony flung his coat on his chair, threw his briefcase on the desk and then swung round and began to eyeball Sam with intent. Sam, who didn't know the man, had no idea that he was only trying to put him at ease.

'I like the cut of this cunts jib,' Tony said in an unusually playful style.

'Why don't you take this cunt out on a job, see how the cunt handles himself?'

Sam was beginning to feel suspicious. Tony looked like the kind of guy that would collapse your pharynx as some form of crude practical joke, and then get confused as to why you were so upset. Where Tony had just instructed Johnny Cheung to take him Sam's mind was only too unhappy to imagine. Despite this, he got up and followed Johnny Cheung. As they left, Tony began to look through old case files as though he were doing work. He wasn't.

\#

Johnny Cheung led Sam to the black Mercedes parked in the street outside. He started the engine and began to rev it furiously.

Sam opened the passenger door and got in. There was barely enough time to shut it again before Johnny Cheung had slammed the car into gear and sped off, the wheels spinning with a hideous screech. The smell of burnt rubber filled the air and Sam's heart beat faster and faster.

Johnny Cheung was pushing the machine ever harder, weaving in and out of traffic, swerving past oncoming cars and cyclists. He was from Hong Kong originally and had been a respected police officer for more than ten years with a reputation for getting results. He thought nothing of cutting up his fellow drivers or forcing people out of his way. It was just the way it was in Hong Kong. Johnny Cheung had always assumed things were the same here, irrespective of sensory information to the contrary. This of course led Sam's journey to be an adrenaline trip he could have done without.

#

Johnny Cheung and Sam pulled up at an ordinary looking semi-detached house. The garden, once well kept, was now getting quite overgrown.

Johnny Cheung rang the doorbell. There was some clattering and Sam could hear heavy footsteps getting closer to the door. Johnny Cheung started to look impatient, he rang again, and the door finally opened.

Sam and Johnny Cheung were confronted by a short, weedy looking man of about forty whose hygiene was questionable to say the least. The man hadn't shaved for some time, his long-matted hair was dripping with grease, and he almost certainly hadn't washed recently. He wore dirty, crumpled clothes and the skin of his arms, hands, bare feet, and face were covered in open sores. There was a fresh cut just below his eye and a line of blood was running down his face, drops of which were rolling from his chin and splattering onto his foot. From time to time, he flicked his tongue out at this dribble of blood, collecting up a sample which he then drew back into his mouth, swilling it around with a look of pleasure, as if he were tasting a fine wine. This action also allowed Sam to notice the man's teeth, which were black and rotten, leaving him resembling a hideous mutant from a low budget horror film. More shocking than the man's appearance, was the smell. Even Johnny Cheung was aghast, and this was a man who had once chased a suspect all the way into the depths of the Hong Kong sewerage system. Seven million people's shit all concentrated into the one place, in the heart of summer as well. The shit, combined with the heat, had produced a stench so foul it would have forced even the most hardened coprophile to vomit. Yet Johnny Cheung had taken this all in his stride, barely flinching as he ran waist deep in the whole city's filth.

Sam's olfactory senses were not amused either. He had turned around and was using his nicotine scented hand wrapped around his face as some sort of tobacco flavoured air freshener.

'Get your stuff quick,' the man whispered. 'We don't have much time. I'm being watched night and day.' He looked around. 'I see things... you see? That's why I am being watched,' he looked around again. 'I'm very important you know?' the man added with a smile, feeling very proud.

Sam had serious reservations about this last statement. He was wondering what the best approach would be as Johnny Cheung went to get the equipment from the boot of the Mercedes. Looking for devices and then, when none were found telling the man the truth. That's what he should do, but that might get the man suspicious. Perhaps it would be better to pretend that they did find some bugs. At least then the man would think that they were being truthful.

Johnny Cheung returned with his kitbag. Sam could tell that the smell had hit him once more. Johnny Cheung's face had scrunched up and his head reeled back. Sam, who had not left the stench, was becoming accustomed to it now.

'Here, you take this,' Johnny Cheung said to Sam as he handed him a contraption not dissimilar to a television remote, but with more dials and displays.

The man watched them excitedly. 'Hurry,' he said. 'Get to work quick as you can.'

Sam and Johnny Cheung stepped into the hall, following the man's lead. The place hadn't been cleaned for a long time, although clearly it had once been subjected to a respectable lady's touch. Watercolour prints of dogs on the wall, small ornamental models of cottages on the coffee table by the sofa, where a delightful vase could also be found.

There was a collection of old shoes and bags of rubbish now lying about on the hallway floor, making it quite an obstacle course.

'Okay, let me show you what to do,' Johnny Cheung told Sam as they stepped around the mess. He held up his own remote control like device and began to explain. 'This is the Evotech401debugger. Very simple. Even a complete idiot could use it.'

Sam hoped this wasn't one of those times where someone says something is simple, just so they can make you feel even more stupid when you fuck things up.

'You press this button and hold it down.' Johnny Cheung continued, pressing a button on his Evotech401debugger. A green LED lit up and the needle of one of the dials wobbled back and forth until it came to rest in the middle, reading 0.00.

Sam whipped out his Evotech401debugger and held down the same button. The green light came on and the dial read 0.00.

'Okay, good,' Johnny Cheung nodded encouragingly to Sam. 'Now you point it at every surface in every room. It doesn't have much range, about two square foot, so you have to be thorough. If it detects a bug, the green light goes off and the red-light flashes, okay?'

'Right.'

'It doesn't beep or anything, so that if people are listening, they don't know you are looking.'

'Right.'

'Did you say people were listening?' the man piped up. Sam and Johnny Cheung ignored him.

'Search in every room and come and get me if you find anything.'

Johnny Cheung turned around to face the man, who was now staring blankly at the wall, lost in thought. Johnny Cheung tapped him on the shoulder, 'I need to examine your electrical equipment. You own a computer?'

'Yes, I built it myself. It's really good. I made it so I could track them.' Johnny Cheung glanced over at Sam and shrugged.

'Follow me,' the man said with an enthusiastic tone, practically skipping through the clutter. 'Here it is,' the man's face was beaming with pride.

Johnny Cheung looked for a moment at what the man was suggesting was his computer. He had made it himself and it wasn't a computer. What it was, was a pile of crap soldered together, badly. Old calculators, radios, clocks, and other broken electrical appliances. It looked like all the prizes from a cheap television game show had gone berserk and gotten into some sort of fight with the tools from the D.I.Y show being filmed in the studio next door. Johnny Cheung rolled his eyes and walked back into the living room. 'I'll just work on the TV for the moment.' He shook his head as he knelt down. He unpacked his tools and got to work taking the TV apart for him to check for bugs.

Sam, feeling that itch between his arse cheeks again, decided to chance his arm. 'Excuse me sir, where is your bathroom?'

The man started looking round nervously, up, down, left, right. He began muttering to himself and shaking his head erratically.

'I need to check for bugs,' Sam said as he brandished the device Johnny Cheung had given him.

'Oh yes, bugs,' the man said, seeming to snap out of whatever delusion he was having. 'Up the stairs and on the left.'

The bathroom was furnished with the same old woman style as the hallway. More pictures of dogs, little ornaments, and an array of different coloured, and probably different scented, soaps in a little basket on the windowsill.

Sam pulled his trousers down and sat on the toilet with a sigh of relief. He grabbed a couple of sheets of toilet paper and wiped hard and deep. It felt good, really good; like scratching an insect bite or pulling a large, gooey lump of clotted snot from your nostril. Sam finished cleaning himself and hoped he had done it properly this time. He went to the sink to wash his hands when he noticed the scene of gore it contained. In addition to blood, there were several scalpels, surgical scissors, tweezers and a couple of other pieces of surgical equipment which Sam did not recognise. There was enough in there to perform a couple of minor operations, and perhaps a few larger ones if you really had to.

More terrifying than the surgical equipment though was the set of sinister looking dentistry tools, which included a whole bunch of those drills dentists always seemed so keen on.

#

Two hours later and Sam had finished sweeping the whole house. Each new room Sam had checked yielded nothing in the way of listening devices. There was plenty of rubbish though. Some rooms were packed full of black bin bags of household waste, others had stacks of old newspapers and magazines. The man must never throw anything out, or at least not very often.

Johnny Cheung had finished disassembling and then reassembling all the electrical appliances in the house and Sam found him in the sitting room, sitting.

'Finished,' Sam said. 'Didn't find a single thing.'

'No, me neither,' Johnny Cheung said apathetically. He looked over at the man, who was sat curled up in the corner of the room, rocking backwards and forwards with his fingers in his ears. 'It doesn't surprise me,' Johnny Cheung said to Sam. 'There isn't anyone watching this guy. Look at him. Who wants to watch him? Maybe some doctors, but even they must have gotten bored. He wouldn't be out otherwise.'

Sam looked at the man, he was indeed a terrible sight and he felt pity for him. At some point the man had someone to look after him, care for him, love him. This looked like it had once been his mother's house. She was gone now, dead probably. The man should be in a hospital, somewhere he really could be watched. Sam resolved that later that day he would try to do something for him, get him some help, get him into a home or something.

'Finished,' Johnny Cheung said to the man, tapping him gently on the shoulder. 'We didn't find anything anywhere in the house.'

The man jumped out of his trance. Johnny Cheung took out a special notepad and wrote a bill, which he handed to the man.

'Umm... is it alright if I pay in cash?' the man asked after examining the bill for a moment. 'I know what happens to all the records if you use credit cards or checks. They watch them you know. They would probably watch you a bit as well, but mostly they would watch me, and my records.'

The man disappeared off into the study, some rustling could be heard and then he reappeared clutching a screwed-up ball of cash in his hand. 'Here you go,' the man said as he handed it over to Johnny Cheung. 'But there is still one place you haven't searched yet.' The man began to strip off his clothes revealing his weedy frame and many more cuts, all over his body. 'I try to get them out but it's hard to find them all. They put them in me when I'm asleep. I try not to sleep but it's hard, I just nod off sometimes, then I have to get them all out, but it's hard to find them all. You must search me with your thing.'

'No problem,' Johnny Cheung said as he waved Sam over to carry out the deed. Sam felt slightly sickened by the prospect of this final search, but considering the disgusting shit he had already put up with today in order to get this job, he thought what the fuck. He took out his Evotech401debugger and switched it on once more. Sam began running the debugger over the man's body, the man was watching him intently.

Being this close, Sam could smell his stench, stronger this time. He sped up, trying to get the ordeal over as quickly as possible. He was done with the top half of the man and was now down to the legs, thighs and buttocks. Sam didn't know who was being degraded more, himself or the man. In any normal circumstances, it would be the man, but this was not any normal circumstance.

Sam finished and again, he had found absolutely nothing.

'Well?' the man asked expectantly.

'Um… there was nothing. I found nothing.'

'WHAT DO YOU MEAN YOU DIDN'T FIND ANYTHING? THAT'S IMPOSSIBLE.' He grabbed Sam by the throat and squeezed. For such a weedy man he was surprisingly strong. Sam couldn't breathe and his neck started to throb, it seemed as if his blood was going to burst out of his cheeks and his eyes were about to explode.

'You're one of them, aren't you?' the man yelled.

'Ugh nmmm uthug,' Sam spluttered in response.

Sam felt bad about what he was going to have to do, but if he didn't take some form of action he was going to die. Sam swung his right arm over the man's arms and pushed down, pulling the man towards him. He caught the man right on the chin with his elbow, letting off an horrendous crack. The man loosened his grip allowing Sam to push him to the ground.

The man cursed as he writhed about on the floor. Sam rubbed his neck, he gasped for breath, sucking air in as if he were breathing for the first time. Johnny Cheung, who had been calmly monitoring the events from a safe distance and chuckling to himself, stepped over the man and started for the door. 'We best get back to Tony's. We'll tell you more about the job then.'

'Blurgh huhuhrumgh,' Sam mumbled in agreement.

Chapter Six

Ford held the ball up to his chin and contemplated the pins for a moment. He took aim, swung back his bowling arm, and stepped forward. The ball flew off down the alley with surprising speed, almost dropping into the gutter before the powerful spin took hold, swinging it back on target. The ball hit the side of the front pin, knocking them all down with a crack that was music to Ford's ears. Had any professionals been watching, they would have been impressed with the level of skill and precision with which Ford bowled. 'Strike!' Ford quietly roared as he strutted back to his seat.

Sam and Sea-mouse were sat, drinking pastis and paying very little attention to the game in hand.

'Take your turn,' Ford told Sam.

'I will when I've finished my drink.'

'I've finished my drink, I'll take my turn,' Sea-mouse said, downing what little was left in his glass.

'No, you won't,' Ford said firmly. 'It's not your go, you'll ruin this game as well if you start getting out of turn again.'

Ford often took Sam and Sea-mouse bowling with him. He saw it as a good social venue, slightly more respectable than the bars and pubs the pair normally haunted. For an up-and-coming lawyer, being so keen on bowling was quite unusual. Most people would imagine golf to be the sport for someone like Ford. In fact, Ford hated golf, even though he had a respectable handicap of six. The trouble was, he generally played golf with his superiors at the firm. They were all impressed by Ford's skill, cooing when he played the trickiest of shots to perfection. Of course, Ford's general worminess meant that he just had to let them win. This was great for his career, but it sapped all the fun from the sport. Bowling on the other hand was a game Ford could play to win, because no one important ever played it.

Sam and Sea-mouse didn't mind going with Ford, although they did tend to see the actual business of bowling as an irritating interruption to their drinking.

Ford picked up his own drink and finished what remained. He realised now that there was no point trying to rush them. Sam would roll when he was good and ready and not before, no amount of polite coercion would help that along.

'Does anyone want another drink?' Ford said, obviously knowing that these drunks would.

'Cuba Libre please,' Sam said.

'Yeah I'll have a couple of Cuba Libres too,' Sea-mouse said. 'Ooh, and a pitcher of Guinness please.'

Ford trotted off to the bar, running through his mind the mechanics of carrying back such a large order.

'Are you sure you want to carry on with this job?' Sea-mouse said, catching site of the bruises around Sam's neck again. 'You of all people should know the dangers of pissing these press people off. You've already been strangled. Being a private investigator might not be the wisest move you ever made.'

'It's not that bad,' Sam said.

'These are powerful and dangerous people at the best of times. You're going to be making some serious enemies.'

'Well, maybe that's exactly the reason I should be doing this. Maybe they deserve a taste of their own medicine.'

'Just be careful, that's all I'm saying.'

'Point taken, but it's really not that dangerous. I'm working tonight following David Morgan OBE's showbiz editor. He's going to some do at a private members club in Soho. Going to be all sorts of celebrities, plus I've got expenses so I'm drinking for free.'

'Can I come?' Ford said excitedly as he put the tray of drinks down at the table. 'I've always wanted to go to a glamorous showbiz party.'

'Course you can,' Sam said, bragging slightly. 'You can come as well if you want Sea-mouse. Expenses.'

'Might as well,' Sea-mouse said, having never turned down free booze in his life.

'We have to get there for about 10:30,' Sam said, looking at his watch.

'That gives us plenty of time for a few more games then,' Ford said, 'or perhaps just about finishing this one.'

Sam took the hint, pulled himself up, grabbed a ball and flung it down the alley. Two pins teetered back and forth for a moment and then gently toppled over.

#

An hour and a half later, the three had finished their game of bowling, a few more rounds of drinks, and were en-route to Soho in the back of a cab.

Ford had started up conversation with the driver, who was talking, in what appeared to Sam at least, to be another made up accent from London. Ford had actually started the conversation himself and was now locked into a banal exchange about traffic restrictions.

Sea-mouse took out his hipflask and began to take quick gulps, not offering any around as it was his emergency supply.

The taxi dropped them off, and they walked the remaining hundred yards to Gonzo's, the trendy private members club. There were a few paparazzi lingering outside, saving their film for any big names that might turn up. Their cue to begin hurling insults and dispassionate abuse, anything to get a reaction.

There wasn't much of a queue to get inside. There never really was, mainly due to the club's exclusivity. Even so, the entrance was roped off and guarded. A man mountain was standing outside and a couple of meataxes were hovering on either side of him. It wasn't until Sam got close that he realised who the man-mountain was. The man-mountain recognised them also.

'What are you three fucks doing here?' Riggs said, half chuckling, half sneering.

Riggs was not only a shitehawk, but also a very dangerous man. Something which was unfortunate for most people who ever encountered his titanic frame. He had been a professional unlicensed boxer in his younger days, and the scars of this could still be seen up and down his face. His nose had been broken several times; his ears were now mostly cauliflower. This left Riggs looking like a living caricature of a very violent thug. Which was what he was. He drank in the Hare & Hounds, mostly with hangers on who were petrified of him, utilising the theory that it was better to befriend the enemy than have your fucking teeth knocked out. A good night out for Riggs consisted of necking ten pints and then picking a fight.

'I'm a member,' Sam said uncertainly. Was he really a member?

'You're a member of this place?' Riggs said, sneering again. He had no idea how such a thing could have happened.

'I've got a temporary membership card,' Sam said as he fished it out of his wallet.

Riggs gave it a scornful look and then handed it back to Sam. 'Okay, you can go in,' he said, lifting the rope. 'But you all better not bother any of the rich people, or I'll smash your fucking faces in.'

Sam and Sea-mouse headed straight to the bar while Ford scooted off in search of the Gents.

'What should we have?' Sam asked Sea-mouse. 'It's all on expenses so we should be able to get pretty leathered.'

Sea-mouse studied the bar, examining all the goodies on offer. 'As we're not paying, why don't we get a nice bottle of champagne?'

Sam thought why not, it couldn't cost that much.

'£700 please,' said the barkeep, placing the bottle and glasses on the bar. Sam felt his bowels begin to move and clenched his buttocks. He took out the credit card Tony had given him and offered it to the bartender, trying to avoid eye contact. Sam watched as he swiped the card. The till began to print out the receipt, tic… tic… ticca, which seemed to take forever. Sam was running through his mind exactly how he was going to justify this to Tony. He was allowed reasonable business expenses, and he was told to try and be inconspicuous, to fit in. Everyone else with few exceptions were guzzling champagne by the bucket load. He was within reason to be drinking a bit of champagne.

Tic… Tic… Ticca… Sam continued to watch with bated breath. Tic… Tic… Ticca… Riiip.

'Sign here please sir,' the barman said as he laid the bill in front of Sam, handing him a pen.

By the time Sam had stuffed his copy of the eye-watering bill into his grubby wallet, Sea-mouse had already taken it upon himself to pour three glasses and was sipping daintily from his own flute. Ford joined them at the bar looking a bit shaken up. 'There are people taking drugs in the toilet.'

'Uhuh,' Sam said as he handed Ford his drink.

'They weren't even being subtle about it. Right there, in the toilet, cutting lines of cocaine at the sink. It was just blatant. They were there, just blatantly sniffing the stuff.'

'Uhuh,' Sam said again.

'I tried to get past them to wash my hands, but this ugly bastard told me to fuck off,' Ford continued. 'Do you think we should tell the police?'

Sam shook his head. He was supposed to be getting photos of people taking drugs. The last thing he needed was Ford calling the filth. 'Come on, let's go and get a table instead.'

It was still early and the place was not exactly packed. A few assorted groups of minor celebrities and journalists sat at various tables. A few models and TV starlets hitting the dance floor. The three found themselves a table out of the way of the other clientèle and Sea-mouse poured another round of drinks, finishing off the bottle.

Sam lit up a cigarette and surveyed the room. He was just about to return to the bar when he spotted his target, Ricky Belane, accompanied by a pair of fellow journalists Sam recognised as working for David Morgan OBE.

Ricky Belane and his crew spent a few moments greeting another group of journalists, creeping ever closer towards the toilets.

Sam reached the gents before they did. He found himself a cubicle, locked the door and waited. He took out the miniature camera Johnny Cheung had handed him that morning (the P4 Spymaster4000) and checked it over. He heard the door open, and several people walk in one after the other.

'Where'd you get this stuff?'

'Same guy, should be as good as last night.'

Sam could hear some rustling and the sound of plastic jabbing quickly on marble.

'What you up to tonight Ricky, staying till the end?' someone asked.

'Nah, only going to be here a couple of hours. Enough time to get a bit fucked up, then I'm off to get my balls wet,' came the reply.

The sound of cutting had finished, Sam stood up on the toilet seat as quietly as he could. He leant over the cubicle door slowly so that he could see the group and looked through the view finder of his camera. One of the journalists Sam had recognised earlier handed Ricky a twenty, the other guys were just standing around gawping. It was like a playground and Ricky was the popular kid showing them how to smoke.

Ricky rolled up the twenty and then, in one fluid motion, snuffled the line of coke up his nose.

Sam took a few quick photos.

'Snorrrt.'

Sam took a couple more photos.

'Aah, fucking hell that's good shit,' Ricky said exaggeratedly.

Ricky handed the twenty to one of the others, who proceeded to go through the same process.

Sam was pretty pleased with himself. He took one final photo and then got down from his perch.

Sam's shoe flicked the toilet seat up slightly as he stepped from it, making a sharp clank, his feet thudding firmly to the floor. 'Shit,' Sam mouthed. He wondered what to do for a few seconds, his heart starting to race. He opened the cubicle door and peered out. The group had obviously heard the commotion and were all looking at Sam. Ricky was staring at him with a puzzled look on his face, trying to place where he recognised Sam from.

'What the fuck were you doing?' one of the group asked, still shovelling white powder up his nose.

'I had the runs,' Sam said, unable to think of anything better to say. He swallowed nervously, wondering what they were going to do.

'Anyone want any pills?' someone asked. The others all shrugged their shoulders and went back to their drugs, as if Sam wasn't even there, barely making room for him as he shuffled past.

Chapter Seven

The lift door slid open and Tony stepped into Vince's office with Johnny Cheung following. Gloria was sat at her desk, idly talking to her sister on the telephone while sculpting what appeared to be a snail out of blue tac with one hand, twisting the forefinger of her other hand around the phone cord.

'Go on through,' she told Tony, covering the phone receiver on her shoulder, 'he's waiting for you both.'

She quickly got back to her phone conversation, paying Tony and Johnny Cheung little more attention.

Vince was sat with his feet up on his desk, gulping down coffee and looking at today's paper.

'Have you seen this?' Vince bellowed, not directing his question at anyone in particular.

'Um… no,' Tony answered. Johnny Cheung shook his head.

'There's a fucking great big, two-page story about me sacking my personal assistant because she wouldn't sleep with me.' Vince gestured for Tony and Johnny Cheung to sit down as he necked the remainder of his coffee.

'I should have expected that bitch to go selling her story to the fucking papers.' Vince pressed down on his intercom controls, 'Gloria, can I have another coffee please,' he demanded.

'You know I fired her because she was fucking useless at her job,' Vince said, staring once again at David Morgan OBE's hateful article.

Gloria stepped into the office carrying a tray of refreshments which she dumped on Vince's desk.

'The bitch isn't even suing me,' Vince added as he began to gulp at his fresh coffee, regardless of the temperature. He lit up a cigarette and took a long drag. 'Look what that fuck David Morgan OB bastard E has reduced me to,' Vince said bitterly. 'Smoking again after having quit for nearly a year.' Vince hadn't really quit for nearly a year. He quit for about a week, enjoyed all the praise from friends and colleagues for having such fantastic reserves of willpower, and then started smoking again in secret.

'What a cunt,' Tony said supportively.

'Quite,' said Vince, lighting another one off the end of the last. 'So,' he said a little calmer now. 'What filth have you dug up on these bastards, anything on David Morgan OBE?'

Tony reached into his jacket and pulled out a rolled-up file, which he tossed onto Vince's desk. Vince clearly didn't take too kindly to this method of presenting data, but he wasn't going to say anything, he was still terrified of Tony.

Vince leafed through the pages of notes and surveillance records. He took out the envelope and studied the photos it contained for a while, chuckling to himself at the one of Ricky Belane.

'Right… So we've got a couple of alcoholic food critics, a wife beating sports reporter, and a suicidal agony aunt,' Vince read to Tony, still staring down at the files.

The agony aunt was a particularly tough case to crack. Tony, Johnny Cheung, and Sam had all spent hours sat in the car documenting her tedious life. Listening in on rambling phone calls to the Samaritans, following her on the many trips she took to the park to feed the ducks and drink almost neat gin from an old Ribena bottle. Sam had been forced into rummaging through her bins on a regular basis, which provided a wealth of screwed up, tear stained and apologetic suicide notes, detailing her boredom at the "pointlessness of life" and of her utter hatred for David Morgan OBE. Oh, she despised that man, who bullied her incessantly at work. She hated the whiny readers of her column nearly as much as David Morgan OBE, with their titillating sexual problems and pathetic complaints about friends taking them for granted. They reflected her own self-loathing.

'This is a good starting point,' Vince said after a while. 'But there's nothing really sordid here though!'

'We'll crack this cunt, don't you worry,' Tony said confidently.

'It takes time,' Johnny Cheung chipped in, feeling he ought to make his presence felt at least a bit in this meeting.

'Well, have you ruined any of these bastards' lives yet?'

'Um, we'll be making a start on that cunt soon. Our associate will soon be telling a travel correspondent's husband that it was his wife what gave him the crabs and not the rent boy. Oh, and he'll be doing that special one for David Morgan O.B. Cunting E. tomorrow.'

'Good, good...' Vince paused for a moment. 'You know, I've been having a few ideas about this area,' he said, sounding very confident in his own vision as usual. 'How about we start our own newspaper?'

'A newspaper?' Tony and Johnny Cheung said in unison, sounding very surprised.

'Yeah, we'll make a newspaper with all the stories about journalists you've been digging up.'

'Do you have any idea exactly how much that would cost?' Tony asked quite assertively but with a smile.

Vince hadn't thought about how much it would cost, and he didn't appreciate Tony pointing it out.

'And even if you did manage to make something like that, have you thought about what sort of cunt is going to buy it? I don't think many people are going to care enough about journalists to part with their cash to find out what they've been up to.'

Vince was getting agitated; he hadn't had people criticise his ideas for a long time and he didn't much like it. He got on the intercom and demanded more 'fucking' coffee to show his disapproval at Tony's comments.

'And what are you going to put in this newspaper?' Tony continued. 'Even if we knew every cunting thing every one of these cunts did when they did it, we still wouldn't have enough material to make a whole newspaper more than once a month. You'd be better off spending your money on adverts or some cunting thing, be a whole lot cunting cheaper.'

Vince was at blowing point. His face was turning red and he had snapped his pen from clenching too hard, but something Tony had said had stuck. Adverts… Adverts… Adverts… went ringing through his mind. Then he shouted, Hold on a fucking minute, that's a fucking brilliant idea, I'm a fucking genius!' Vince's mind was on fire. 'I'm seeing billboards, magazines, TV. People will have to see that, and then they'll know, they'll all know, and that Ricky Belane fucker can be first.

Tony looked to Johnny Cheung and he knew that they were both in agreement. 'What a cunt,' they thought in unison.

Chapter Eight

Sam leant against someone's hard, plastic suitcase which made up just part of the mass of bodies and luggage cluttering up the carriage. He was half sitting, half standing, but achieving neither to an extent that could be considered comfortable. Every so often, a sudden jerk of the train caused Sam to knock body parts with the man standing next to him. Something they both seemed to accept.

Sam disliked trains at the best of times, but today's trip had cemented his hatred for them. The whole journey had started out bad and managed to keep this way throughout. As soon as he had bought his ticket, he had been informed that his train was going to be delayed by twenty minutes. It had been more like an hour. Sam was wretchedly hungover and the idea of missing out on extra recovery time for no reason left him cursing the day trains were invented.

There was a battered and abused Coke machine on the platform where Sam had been waiting; probably the station's only amenity unless you considered the few rusty benches scattered around, or Steve, the piss sodden tramp in the car park.

Sam bought himself a drink, hoping it might sooth his throbbing head. The sickly-sweet liquid absorbed itself into the fur growing on his teeth and tongue, forming a good foundation for the layer of tar he was about to set down with his first cigarette of the day. His lungs lit neurons on fire, but the nicotine felt good. Sam began to cough and a lump of something bad tasting came up which he spat out. A man in a smart suit had looked at him and shook his head.

Once Sam had gotten on the train, he felt slightly better. Progress was being made and the worst was probably over. He began to settle into his chair and had even thought about catching up on a little sleep, maybe get through the last of the booze in his blood stream. This hadn't lasted long though. After the second stop, about fifteen minutes actual journey time, an announcement came over the intercom, 'I'm afraid this train will terminate at this station, we apologise for any inconvenience. A bus will take you to some other fucking station and you might be able to continue your fucking journey from there. God willing.' Another half an hour of waiting around had gone by, cigarettes were smoked and a couple more cans of Coke were drunk. All of which started to make Sam's heart do strange and wonderful beats.

There was never any way everyone was going to fit into the coach which finally turned up. Sam found himself standing cramped at the back of the bus, aware that everyone around him could smell his stink of alcohol and it was early enough into this horrific journey for Sam to be embarrassed about it. That would soon pass.

Next station on the list, waiting for what was almost certainly the only train. The platform was packed. Sam had never seen so many people waiting for so little. And he was one of them.

The last great hope had eventually turned up, behind schedule, and everyone piled on.

Sam waited a while to finish the cigarette he had just started before trying to get on the train. Sam was always to be found at the back of the queue. Accept your fate and resign yourself to being uncomfortable and at a disadvantage, and then you can calmly stroll on amongst everyone else, still maintaining a little dignity.

The train was completely full when Sam finally stepped on, flicking his cigarette butt on the dirty platform floor in an act of defiant littering. He pulled his shoulders in and sucked in his chest, trying to make himself as small as possible as he squeezed past his fellow passengers standing in the aisle.

And now, as Sam travelled up the streak of piss that was the British Rail Network, half sitting, half standing on someone's hard, plastic suitcase, Sam couldn't help thinking of the candirú fish; a tiny parasitic catfish which lodges itself in the urethra of any would-be jungle adventurers foolish enough to relieve themselves while having a quick dip in the river. Surgery was the only way to get those little bastards out. Sam started to compose a letter of complaint in his head to the rail company. He knew that no response would ever come from it, but it was going to be a vicious yet witty attack on everything those bastards held dear. It didn't matter that the only person who would ever read it would be some poorly paid worker in customer services, because Sam knew full well that as soon as he got home, he would forget all about it and never even bother to write the thing. It helped to pass the time though, and it helped Sam to go inside of himself, to blank out his uncomfortable surroundings. A sort of meditation for concerned parties. He almost didn't notice when someone compressed his innards with their big fat arse as they pushed past to get to the buffet cart. It would have had to be a very deep meditation for Sam not to notice. He couldn't imagine what kind of idiot would think it a good idea on the most crowded train they're ever likely to see, to smash everyone out of the way just to get a filthy, squalid sandwich from the buffet cart.

#

The train pulled up at Sam's station. Sam looked out of the window and there, above the platform, was a huge billboard of Ricky Belane snorting a line of coke. It had in huge black letters at the bottom "IS THIS WHO YOU WANT IN YOUR MORNING PAPERS?"

Sam overheard a few passengers commenting on how disgusting it was, a man abusing his position like that. Sam had never felt pride about his work before, not when he saw his words in print, or when one of his reports had been read on air. This felt different, this felt like he was actually doing something, actually reaching people and affecting them. He was definitely getting in a couple of people's faces, and best of all, it was people he disliked immensely.

'I get that paper you know,' the gentleman opposite Sam said, presumably to him.

'Uhhuh,' Sam responded trying not to show interest.

'Disgusting, isn't it?' the commuter continued, 'allowing a man like that to write for them.'

Sam nodded and smiled.

Finally, the doors opened with a hiss and people started to leak out.

As he burst out of his metal cocoon of punishment, Sam imagined the sun shining down on his face and a cool fresh breeze drying the beads of sweat dripping from his brow. The sun wasn't and a breeze didn't, but Sam imagined it and it made him feel slightly better. It was almost worth the torture he had just endured these last few hours, just to taste how sweet this freedom finally was. Almost, but not quite.

\#

There was a pub opposite the station and he headed straight for it.

The pub was one of those rough looking holes that could often be found near to train stations. The outside walls even looked grubby and nicotine stained and Sam had a fair idea that it would be much worse on the inside. The windows were the old kind, made of many sections in lead frames. They would have looked quite nice if it wasn't for the fact that most of the glass had been replaced by pieces of chipboard. Or were covered in so much dirt that archaeologists might make some interesting discoveries if they could ever hold a dig long enough without getting stabbed.

Sam didn't really care what the place looked like. They sold alcohol. He pulled at the door and went in. The place was everything Sam had imagined from the outside and much less. The sort of place that was fitted out so cheaply, that it had the look of a village hall rather than a watering hole.

It was only 11:30 in the morning and the bar was practically empty. The barman was a barrel-chested old bastard who clearly wasn't a man to be messed with. His shiny, wrinkled, bald head had several scars which glowed against his orange tan. There were two large gold earrings, presumably stolen from a pirate, hanging down from each ear, stretching his lobes under their weight. The only patron apart from Sam was a grubby old drunk, already halfway through his second pint and rolling a needle thin cigarette while puffing away at the one stuck to his bottom lip.

The barman stared at Sam like he was scum.

'Pint of Guinness, please,' Sam said. The barman barely acknowledged Sam as he went about the motions of pouring his drink. He stuck his hand out for payment without even bothering to mention the price, as if everyone was supposed to know intuitively. Sam chucked a five-pound note on the bar, noticing from his change that the prices were quite reasonable.

Sam took a good, long swig from his pint as he wandered over to the cigarette machine for a fresh deck. He necked some more of his pint; he could feel it hitting his empty stomach wall and leaching into his blood, bringing up his already high blood alcohol level to a point where he was beginning to feel better. He lit up the last smoke from his old packet and felt slightly dirty. His lungs did too. Sam finished the last half of his pint in three mouthfuls and took his glass back over to the bar.

'Same again please, mate,' he choked in between a mouthful of smoke.

The barman took the glass in a disgusted fashion. Like he had been distracted from an important task, which seemed to be watching a fly sick up vomit on a stray peanut at the edge of the drip tray. He filled the used glass up with Guinness, not bothering to let it settle halfway through, and handed it back to Sam. If Ford was with him, he would have probably made some comment about not using a clean glass being against health regulations and a fineable offence. Sam wasn't bothered, he was doing his tiny bit for the environment.

Sam took a hit of his new beer and could really feel the alcohol start to work on his brain. 'This had better be the last one,' he thought to himself, taking another swig and then a drag on his cigarette. He wanted to be slightly drunk, in light of what he was about to do. He couldn't turn up pissed though, he knew that. That would be counterproductive, disrespectful even. Sam didn't have much love for David Morgan OBE. That man was a piece of shit as far as Sam was concerned, but something about this didn't sit right with him. Vince's little something extra for David Morgan OBE felt wrong, very wrong. Sam had sensed that Tony was uneasy about it too. He seemed in two minds when he had given Sam the assignment, like he was glad to be palming this part of the job off onto someone else but still couldn't displace the bitter taste of guilt it left. Ruining people's lives was one thing, but this was possibly going a step too far.

\#

Sam fell out of the pub and opened the shitty photocopied map Tony had given him. The house was clearly marked with red felt tip, and the route from the station was highlighted in lurid fluorescent yellow. It wasn't that far. Just a case of walking out the door, then down the street and boom, he would be there. A few paces in and Sam stood deathly still in the middle of the pavement. It crossed his mind that he didn't have to do this, he could just head home and forget all about the whole thing. It was a flashback of trains more than anything else that spurred Sam back into action. Sam hardly realised that he had arrived at his destination. He was now standing, looking up in awe at the front of David Morgan OBE's mothers' house. It's not that it was an imposing building, it wasn't. It's just what it stood for. The place itself was a magnificent townhouse steeped in history. George IV had once done a maid servant up the arse in the bathroom. He'd also got roaringly drunk after consuming four bottles of port in an hour and then spent a further six hours hopelessly trying to make love to a chaise lounge. Had Sexfiend been better schooled in such matters of history, he may have found himself an idol to look up to and admire. As it was, he was pig ignorant in practically everything. Although, in the spirit of deviancy George IV would have admired, Sexfiend had also done a maid servant up the arse in a bathroom before spending six hours, hopelessly trying to make love to a chaise lounge.

Sam shuddered as he walked up the pathway to the front door. He would have had another cigarette, delaying this for a little while longer, but his heart already felt like it was going to burst out of his chest from nerves and all the nicotine in his system. He was sure that it wasn't normal for a man his age to suffer from palpitations and such an irregular pulse. One of these days he was going to start paying attention to Ford's nagging and take a long, hard look at some of his lifestyle choices.

Sam swung the heavy knocker against the large oak door. He flinched slightly at the booming noise it produced, which seemed to resonate through the whole interior of the house and echoed down the street. Sam tucked his shirt in and tried to tidy up his hair a little while he waited for a response.

'Hello?' Mrs. Morgan said as she opened the door, sizing Sam up but still maintaining a pleasant, welcoming smile on her face.

'Hi… Um… Mrs. Morgan?'

'Yes,' she replied cautiously.

'Hi, Mrs. Morgan. I'm… I was… Um… Um… I'm supposed to um… I'm here… Um… to talk to you a little about your son, David Morgan OBE.'

Her smile widened, showing off a perfect set of pearly white teeth and her bright, hazelnut eyes lit up. 'You're a friend of my David are you?' Sam didn't get a chance to reply. 'Do come in won't you, I was just making some herbal tea.' She had already opened the front door wide and was heading back into the house.

Sam could do nothing but follow. He stepped inside, shutting the door behind him as Mrs. Morgan waltzed off down the hall.

Sam had to rush to keep up with her as she was really racing down the corridor to the sitting room. Several magnificent paintings adorned the walls and Sam thought he recognised the styles of Constable in a couple, possibly a Turner too. He was pretty sure he recognised an early piece by Freud hanging by the stairway, but he wasn't a hundred percent sure on that one. As a student, Sam often liked to wander around museums and art galleries; he found the ambience of such places good for nasty hangovers. He'd moved on to garden centres in recent years, but the effect was still the same, although not as educational.

'Mind you don't stand there,' Mrs. Morgan said, pointing to an expensive looking Turkish rug and carefully skirting around it.

She led him into a large sitting room, beautifully decorated with masterpieces. Large Chinese vases by the window, a French mahogany drinks cabinet in the corner. The wall immediately facing the vases had three paintings which looked very much like the work of Picasso in his cubist period. The walls on either side both had paintings, but Sam couldn't even guess at what they were, besides expensive.

Mrs. Morgan directed Sam to sit down on a large antique sofa, which he did. A collector might consider the piece exquisite had it not been for the lace armrest covers, clearly made by herself and not to a particularly high standard. Mrs. Morgan moved a pile of embroidery magazines to a slightly worn-out looking chaise lounge and sat herself down with a satisfied sigh on another sofa opposite Sam.

'So nice of you to come and visit me,' she told Sam, looking at him pleasantly. 'David often sends someone to see me if they're up this way. He's such a thoughtful boy. I so rarely have guests anymore.'

'Um… yes, about that,' Sam said.

'He knows how I like company, and most of my friends are gone now, God rest their souls.'

'Yes, about David,' Sam said. It was beginning to get painful for him now.

'He phones me every day when he's away in the city.'

'It's David I want to talk to you about, Mrs. Morgan…'

'Ooh, wait a minute,' Mrs. Morgan said, jumping out of her seat, 'I'll just go and see to that tea.'

Before Sam could say any more, she had swept out of the room with such amazing grace Sam imagined that she must have spent time as a thespian. He was a little relieved that he had been left alone for a while. At least he could have some time to work out how he was going to tell her.

Mrs. Morgan returned carrying a tray with two incredibly expensive bone china cups of tea and some scones she had made herself only this morning. Mrs. Morgan always made scones in the morning. If she didn't have any guests during the day, the birds were always sure to be grateful for them. Mrs. Morgan had the most foppishly English birds living in her garden. If they had opposable thumbs, they might have fashioned themselves little monocles and top hats. As it was, they just pecked around the bird feeder a bit and shat on her washing.

Something Sam noticed, as Mrs. Morgan plonked the tea down and wafted back into her seat, was that she had managed to find time to apply a pea green face mask to herself whilst she was making the brew.

She caught him staring, even though Sam was trying to be subtle. 'Oh this deary,' she said innocently. 'If I don't apply this gunk every six hours, my skin feels just wretched. You know how silly old women are.'

'I wouldn't say you were old Mrs. Morgan,' Sam said, trying to flatter her a bit, in light of the terrible thing he was about to do.

'Ooh stop,' she giggled, smiling at Sam.

Mrs. Morgan had, for almost all her life, been completely obsessed about her age. It's not that she wanted to be young forever; it's just that she wanted to look good forever. The secret of looking good, as far as Mrs. Morgan could tell, was all down to the skin. Your hair could grow grey and your voice could become haggard, but as long as your skin was still smooth and supple, you would remain looking good. This was the reason for Mrs. Morgan's strict face mask regime. Less noticeable was her religious hand cream applications. It wasn't just her hands that she applied the most expensive of moisturisers to, but her entire body also. Nine o'clock every evening and her chest would be basted, mornings it would be her legs. In the afternoon she would lather her trunk. For someone so concerned with her looks, it might be thought that Mrs. Morgan would spend a lot of money on expensive plastic surgery. She didn't. Mrs. Morgan thought that sort of thing was for amateurs only. If you wanted to look good, and stay looking good for as long as possible, you had to stay away from anything temporary. Stay out of the sun or tanning salons, it ages the skin. Facelifts don't last, and more than that, they look wrong. Ridiculous even. To keep your skin nice, you must take good care of it, nurture it. Like a bonsai tree which can remain beautiful for hundreds of years.

It wasn't out of narcissism that Mrs. Morgan was so obsessed with her looks; it was more of a hobby. Mrs. Morgan's mother had always told her that everyone needed something as way of a distraction from the pressures and pains of life. Some people collect stamps, some people build model planes, and others buy lots of shoes. For Mrs. Morgan, she had her skin.

What started as a simple hobby soon became an obsession and took up most of her spare time. Friends and remaining family once thought that Mrs. Morgan had taken up jogging as a hobby instead and for a while it did seem like that. But that wasn't so; she had only taken up jogging after reading a book about Einstein's special theory of relativity. The way Mrs. Morgan understood it, the closer an object gets to the speed of light, the slower time will go for that object. A light bulb directly above Mrs. Morgan's head blew at the exact moment she learned this nugget of information. She now quite literally had a way to slow the progress of time for herself, and it had a one hundred percent guarantee from a genius. Everyone around her would grow old and look worse and worse, but not her. She would stay the same from now on. It was all a question of keeping herself moving, and she threw herself into this with all of the passion she had put into discovering new skin treatments or raising David. Instead of walking, she would run. Instead of driving down to the shops, she drove really fucking fast down to the shops, trading her old hatchback for a sporty little number. Instead of sleeping in her bed, she slept in a large industrial centrifuge. This new fad didn't last long though, only a few weeks. She soon realised that she wasn't getting close enough to the speed of light (299,792,458 m/s) to have any real effect. Just a few seconds, that was all Mrs. Morgan thought she had saved herself. It just didn't add up. She realised that she was probably ageing a lot more what with all the extra sweating and gurning from over exertion, which was bound to be having a negative effect on her skin. So Mrs. Morgan gave up on physics, although she still went on as many long-distance flights as she could.

'This tea is good for the skin you know, my lovely,' she added, taking dainty sips of her steaming green brew, which looked a lot like a diluted version of the crap she had on her face. Sam had a try of his tea, unconsciously poking his pinkie out as he raised the cup to his mouth, the bitter, watery drink almost making him wretch. He nearly choked again when he began to tell Mrs. Morgan why he was actually here.

'Umm... About David, Mrs. Morgan,' he stuttered.

'Yes dear?' she said with a proud look in her eyes, as if she was expecting to receive serious praise about her son.

'Um… well, this may seem like an odd question.'

'Yes?'

'Well, um, do you remember that brooch your grandmother gave you? The one that's been in your family for generations and was originally a present to your great, great grandmother from the second Earl of Rochester?' Mrs. Morgan's expression changed dramatically. There was a mixture of surprise and sadness in equal proportions as she remembered that brooch, a most treasured heirloom. 'Yes, I remember it,' she said, shooting Sam a suspicious look while maintaining her friendly smile.

'And you remember how you sold it at auction to pay for David's school fees?'

Mrs. Morgan blushed, although no one but her could tell under all of that expensive, seaweed exfoliant.

'Yes, I remember that too,' she sighed. She remembered also how she had sobbed herself to sleep for months after the sale, losing the only possession she ever really cared about had been a very painful experience for Mrs. Morgan. She missed her granny's brooch, but she didn't regret selling it. It hadn't been a hard decision to make, it had to be done. She wanted the best for her son, and selling her most valuable possession allowed her to give him the best. No good would have come from David being punished for the mistakes made by his lousy father.

'Why exactly are you telling me all of this?' Mrs. Morgan asked, her patience starting to wear thin, but only a little. 'David didn't send you round just to keep me company, did he? What's going on?'

Sam tried to think how he should explain all of this. He took a manila envelope out of his jacket pocket and began toying with it in his hands; his sticky sweat began to soak into the paper leaving dark patches.

'Um,' he said. He took a mouthful of the foul-tasting tea, hoping that it would clear his throat.

'Well?' Mrs. Morgan asked.

'Well, about that brooch, Mrs. Morgan.'

'Yes?'

Sam looked like he was straining to take a shit. 'Well... David you see.'

'Yes?'

'Well, he's managed to track it down,' Sam finally blurted out.

'What?' Mrs. Morgan practically screamed in a high-pitched falsetto.

'He's found it,' Sam continued. 'You thought it was lost forever, even tried to find it yourself but it had changed hands. No one seemed to know where it had gone. Well, David's found it. He's spent over a year searching for it, but now he's found it and he's bought it for you.'

Mrs. Morgan was stunned. It was a lot of information to take in and she couldn't quite work out what was going on. She did feel very proud of her son. There was something though, that wasn't quite right about all of this.

'I don't understand. If he's gone to so much trouble over this, why hasn't he come here to give it to me in person?'

'Well, um, he bought it for you, and… he was going to give it you for Christmas, as a surprise,' Sam told her as quickly as he could, clearly uncomfortable. He took out a couple of grainy photos of David Morgan OBE examining the brooch in a jewellers. 'Look, see,' he said, passing one over to Mrs. Morgan.

She didn't look at the photo, she was staring at Sam in disbelief. 'If David wanted it to be a surprise, why are you telling me this? Christmas is months away.' There was more confusion in her voice than anger, but that would soon change.

'Well, I'm supposed to tell you that too.' Sam wanted to die. At this very moment, he wished that there would be a huge earthquake or something and he would be swallowed up into a deep, dark hole of molten rock where he would be burned alive. That would be preferable to this. Mrs. Morgan was glowering at him, she hadn't blinked for some time now.

'You see, umm… I work for a private detective and um… I was hired by someone who really doesn't like your son. I mean, he really hates him.'

Mrs. Morgan was aghast; she had never thought it possible that someone would dislike David.

Sam tried to continue, 'and um… I was hired to… um… follow your son around, so I… So I could tell you what you were getting for Christmas and um… ruin the surprise. I'm sorry.' Sam felt relieved for finally getting this out, although the worst was probably still to come.

'Someone paid you to ruin Christmas for me?' she cried.

'Yes. I'm sorry. We didn't know we would be ruining something so big, we all thought it would be bath salts or something.'

'Why?' she asked. Mrs. Morgan couldn't imagine why anyone would do this. This wouldn't be excusable for someone to do to the mother of a mass murderer or child rapist. But to do something so cold, so vindictive to her, she just couldn't get her head round. As far as Mrs. Morgan was concerned, David was a successful journalist and now a high-flying editor of the country's most popular newspaper. She didn't read it herself; it was a little lowbrow for her. But still, it was something to be very, very proud of.

'This is sick,' she starting to raise her voice. 'You're sick, you're disgusting. Whoever hired you is disgusting.' She tried to stop herself but she couldn't, bursting into a flood of tears like never before.

Sam wanted to burst into tears too, but he didn't, he just sat there whimpering and staring at his shoes. 'I'm sorry,' he said again, as humbly as he could.

Mrs. Morgan leapt up, grabbing her cup of herbal tea, and threw the contents in Sam's face. In her mind, it was boiling hot, in reality, the tea had cooled. It was tepid, quite tepid. 'Get out,' she screamed, 'get out of my house, you animal.'

Mrs. Morgan was sat back down again now, sobbing into her hands, looking almost as if she was praying. Sam got up and began to leave. 'I'll see myself out,' he said quietly, trying not to disturb her in case she attacked him.

'Just get out.'

Sam sped up, practically running out of the house. He fell out onto the street, shutting the front door behind him. He wished there was someone else with him. Johnny Cheung or Sea-mouse, or even Ford. Someone that he could say 'well that went well' to and then they could both laugh nervously. But no one was with him. He was all alone and he wasn't laughing. He lit up a smoke and decided he might as well go back to that pub for a couple of hours. If he was going to have to get the train back, Sam thought it would be best to be out of his mind.

Chapter Nine

'Yes mum, I know,' David Morgan OBE said down the telephone in a calm, soothing voice, masking the rage and fury embedded deep inside. His face had gone red and his teeth were clenched. A vein on David Morgan OBE's forehead was throbbing. David Morgan OBE hadn't been this close to having an aneurism since that prolonged bout of constipation a few years back. That was brought on by stress too, although he would have to wait and see if this incident was going to disrupt his bowel movements.

'Look mum, I've really got to go now… I'll be coming round tonight though so I might as well bring the broach with me.' He ripped one of the balls from his executive play toy and threw it in the bin. The rest of the balls were no longer clacking properly so he picked the whole thing up and threw that in the bin too, even more aggressively.

'Yes, I know mum, but there doesn't seem much point waiting until Christmas now.' He drew a small tanto dagger on the notepad next to the phone and then crossed it out with sharp, violent slashes of his pencil, snapping it in the process. He picked the notepad and pencil up and threw them in the bin too.

'Yes mum… Okay, I'll see you tonight… Okay mum, I'll see you tonight… I love you too… Okay, bye… yes, bye… love you.'

He slammed down the receiver after listening for his mum clicking off. That wasn't enough. He scooped up the phone and pulled, hoping to wrench the whole thing out of the socket. The cable was longer than David Morgan OBE gave it credit for. Not to be deterred, he wound up what of the wire he could and then ran backwards out of the open office door, pulling all the way. The journos in the open plan office outside of David Morgan OBE's personal suite stared at him, amazed and bewildered. They all knew he was in a bad mood, it could only be expected at a time like this, but David Morgan OBE was behaving very strangely. More so than normal. David Morgan OBE finally found the resistance of the end of the cord at about twenty feet, next to some nobody advert pushers' desk. The nobody advert pusher was helplessly trying to beg another square inch of space out of some nobody carpet warehouse. He was too busy pleading and worrying about his job to notice David Morgan OBE, who was also busy and wouldn't have noticed the nobody advert pusher even if he wasn't.

David Morgan OBE fell backwards, landing on his arse as the phone was finally ripped from its socket. He was quick to get himself back up, running towards his office and screaming wildly, holding the phone above his head with outstretched arms, as if he had just won a prize. He ran up to the bin by his desk and threw the phone into it with all the force he could muster, screaming even more wildly than before.

He stormed back out into the main office area. 'Do you know what those fucking cunts have done now?' he shouted to no one in particular. 'If anyone is going to ruin Christmas, it's going to be me.'

Not a single person in the room wanted to make eye contact with the beast. They looked around shiftily at their feet or pretended to get on with some work. The idea of ritualised self-disembowelment had never been less appealing with David Morgan OBE in a mood like this.

This had probably been the worst day at work David Morgan OBE could remember, and there had been some tough times in the past. Libel cases, death threats, deaths, poor circulation figures, lack of any decent cover story for the next day's issue, presses going haywire, and worst of all, being beaten to a scoop by a rival. This, what this was, this was uncharted territory, and David Morgan OBE didn't like it one bit.

'Has that idiot Belane killed himself yet?' David Morgan OBE asked his PA. She looked a bit worried, as if it would be her neck if she gave the wrong answer. Everyone else had gotten back to work, each and every one of them hoping that they wouldn't be singled out.

'Um... No. I don't think he has,' she said, checking through some memos on her desk.

'Are you sure?'

'Fairly sure sir, he's been writing his column from the stationery cupboard downstairs for the last week, since you spoke… yelled at him about those signs.'

David Morgan OBE looked relieved for a few seconds, then became slightly disgruntled, scratching his head for an imaginary itch. 'Didn't I fire him?'

'No sir, you just shouted at him for quite a while and strongly recommended the cleaner to act as a second. Good strong arm on her you thought, probably from all that mopping. "Take your head clean off with one good strike" you said.'

David Morgan OBE thought about this for a while. At the time he had really hoped Ricky Belane would have done the decent thing and committed hara-kiri, but it was probably just as well that he hadn't. Now, more than before, David Morgan OBE needed to find out everything he could about what's been going on. 'Find the prick and send him my way. And feel free to make any comments you like about his dress sense and the size of his manhood that you feel necessary.'

#

David Morgan OBE left his PA to make some calls. He headed back into his office and sat down at his desk. He looked at the mess he had made and sighed. He retrieved the phone from the bin and plugged it back in. David Morgan OBE thought about tidying things up a bit more, but instead he opened up his desk drawer and took out a small gold coloured cardboard box. A dim glow seemed to emanate from it, as if it were sucking up the light and spitting it back out. He rubbed a finger over it softly and smiled; it felt new, it felt good. He opened it up and took out his mum's brooch, it seemed a lot grander than he remembered it as a kid. The white gold had blackened slightly with age but that just seemed to add to the charm. It was sculpted in the shape of a rose, emeralds decorating the three leaves sprouting off from the stem and the flower was embedded with four perfectly cut rubies, with one larger stone in the middle. It sparkled the colour of blood. For a moment, it seemed to David Morgan OBE that the flower was alive as he played with it in his fingers.

He pinned it onto his lapel and looked at his reflection in the window. He scolded himself for being so silly and quickly unclipped the brooch, putting it back into its box. He took a card out of the drawer and grabbed a pen. It was a handmade card and David Morgan OBE had commissioned his mother's favourite wildlife artist to paint a picture of a cat on the front. He opened it up and began to write, 'To my darling mother, from your loving son who will never be able to repay in full everything you sacrificed for me. David XXX.' Anyone else reading that would probably either gag or laugh, but not his mother. A tear began to form around David Morgan OBE's eye, before slowly rolling down his face. He dabbed his finger on it lightly and plucked it off. It hadn't broken; a perfectly formed droplet was still wobbling on the tip of his forefinger. David Morgan OBE couldn't remember the last time he had cried. He was sure he had at some point, when he was a baby at least, he just couldn't remember now. He hadn't cried when he was told that his father was dead, he remembered that clearly, almost with pride, but now, once one had formed, more tears came until he began to whimper in full snotty helplessness as a lifetime of tears flooded out. He no longer felt angry anymore, just sad.

The phone began to ring, disturbing David Morgan OBE's wallowing just as he was starting to get going. He pulled himself together, wiping his tears on his pocket handkerchief, removing the watery snot from his nostrils with one deep, powerful breath in.

He picked up the phone, it was his PA, 'Belane is here, he looks terrible.'

David Morgan OBE took a second to get his mind back on track. 'Okay, send that prick in,' he muttered, still concentrating hard on removing all memory of what he had just been doing.

'Okay you stupid fuck,' David Morgan OBE screamed as Ricky Belane tentatively crept through the door. 'Sit down and don't say a fucking word until I tell you to.'

Ricky Belane sat down and cowered. The last time Ricky Belane had seen David Morgan OBE it hadn't gone too well and he had no false expectations that this would go any better.

'Okay you… you prat,' David Morgan OBE said, starting to gather speed and focus, 'I'm not mad at the photos anymore,' he lied. 'What's done is done. What's important to me now is that you remember everything you can about when these pictures could have been taken.' David Morgan OBE hadn't even asked Ricky Belane about this last time, he was too busy cursing. 'We need to find out who is doing this to us. Whoever they are, they've gone too far, too fucking far for sure.' David Morgan OBE was glowing red with rage again and it felt good. He was starting to get back to his old self.

Ricky Belane had been thinking about those photos of him for some time now. Not only had they put him in this messy situation, but now everyone was talking about it behind his back. Everywhere he went people would be pointing at him, jeering at him, even swearing at him. His parents had been trying to phone him since the billboards first appeared but he hadn't been answering, he just couldn't face them. He also couldn't face all the people who had been phoning him since the billboards appeared, just to laugh at him. People he'd annoyed along the way, celebrities, celebrity's friends and family, and pretty much anyone who had actually met him, they were all queuing up to get back at him. The only thing that kept him from erasing all the messages that were getting left without listening to them was that it was actually quite good fun trying to work out the numerous celebrities from their thinly disguised voices.

The biggest problem for Ricky Belane was that the photograph could have been taken any night of the week over the last few years. Pretty much since starting his showbiz column that was what he did, every evening. That had all changed now. He hadn't been back to Gonzo's since he first saw the pictures and he'd also sold all of his cocaine to friends. He had thought about flushing it all down the toilet but then reconsidered, expecting that very soon he may be out of a job.

There was one thing that did seem to keep circulating in his mind though. A memory, a shadow, a drunken ghost that seemed to linger through the drug haze of one of those nights. He couldn't quite put his finger on it, but there was definitely someone he remembered who just seemed out of place, but oddly familiar. Someone in the business maybe. Ricky Belane had been racking his brains about this guy for days, he could barely sleep. It was close, he was sure it would come to him; he just had to run through his mind all of the losers he had met at parties or conferences or company days out.

'I'm close sir, just give me a chance. I'll remember something, I swear.'

David Morgan OBE liked Ricky Belane's grovelling. He always enjoyed a good grovelling.

'You have one-week Belane.' He didn't state what the consequences would be if Ricky Belane didn't come up with something. He didn't need to. Just the way he said it sent shivers down his spine. Ricky Belane was imagining things far worse than David Morgan OBE could have planned. The human mind is always at its most creative when imagining all the bad things that could be done to its mode of transport.

'You won't regret it sir,' Ricky Belane said looking slightly to the left of David Morgan OBE's face, still unable to face him head on. 'Just let me check a few things out and I'll be back to you. I won't let you down, I promise.'

'You already have, you shit,' David Morgan OBE muttered. It had gone again; his heart just wasn't in it at the moment. He mustered the last of his energy reserves and stared squarely at Ricky Belane. 'Go on, get out,' he said, nodding towards the door.

Belane walked backwards a few paces, almost bowing before scuttling out.

Chapter Ten

Sam lay in bed as still as he could. If he moved, even a fraction, then the whole room began to spin, and spin, and spin. He heard that knock again, the one that had woken him up way too early, and kept on waking him up every time he tried to get back to sleep. It still hadn't gone away.

Sam rolled out of bed and immediately regretted it. He bravely opened his eyes and immediately regretted that too. 'Ungh,' he groaned painfully in response to a new bout of knocking.

Sam carefully stumbled out of his room, although not carefully enough as he almost knocked over the plastic bottle half full with piss, which had been standing on the floor beside his bed.

'Take your time, did you just get up or something?' Sea-mouse said with a smile as Sam finally opened the door. 'Drink,' he offered Sam, holding up a can of lager, 'they're cold.'

'No thanks,' Sam said hoarsely; he had smoked way too much last night and combined with mild dehydration, it was quite painful to speak.

Sea-mouse opened himself one and took a long slug. A very long slug, he emptied the can. Sea-mouse wiped his mouth with the back of his hand and grinned.

'Are you coming in then?' Sam asked.

Sea-mouse opened another can and took a quick swig. 'That's just it. I'm going to have to get going soon, I'm working tonight.'

Sam looked Sea-mouse over and realised that something was different. He was dressed strangely for a start; a smart suit but no tie, with the top three buttons of his shirt undone leaving his chest exposed but for a cheap gold medallion. Sea-mouse was also wearing a wig, replacing his own blonde mop with dirty brown spikes and just the hint of a mullet. Resting on Sea-mouse's face was a pair of black, thick rimmed plastic glasses.

'Who are you supposed to be?' Sam asked.

A few years ago, Sea-mouse had wandered in off the street into some professional look-a-like agency's office to see if he could use their bathroom. The only person who had been in there was a sleazy looking guy sat flicking paper clips from his desk into the wastepaper bin. As soon as he saw Sea-mouse he was hired. 'Hey kid, you're hired,' he had told Sea-mouse with forced enthusiasm. 'We could use a big guy like you.'

It was the perfect job for a man about town like Sea-mouse. Half the time, Sea-mouse had absolutely no idea who the person was supposed to be. Sea-mouse just showed up, collected his cheque and acted like he owned the place. He let the imagination do the rest.

'Don't know,' Sea-mouse said in answer to Sam's question, 'but he dresses like a complete cunt!'

Sam laughed as he tried to figure out Sea-mouse's costume but just couldn't. An actor from the seventies, a porn star with a freakishly large penis. God knows.

'Seriously though,' Sea-mouse said, 'I don't have much time anymore before I have to be there so we're going to have to get going if you want to come.'

'What time is it?' Sam asked, beginning to feel slightly confused as he noticed that it was starting to get dark.

'It's nearly seven in the evening,' Sea-mouse said with joke disgust, making an annoying clicking sound with his cheek.

Sam didn't feel quite as refreshed as he thought he should after a whole day's R and R. 'Just give me a couple of minutes while I change my shirt and brush my teeth,' he said as he headed back into the house.

\#

Sam and Sea-mouse stepped into the party, which was being held in a club downtown. They had walked there, it hadn't been that far, stopping only once for refreshments in a pub on the way. They still managed to get to the place within lateness specifications. Sea-mouse was instructed, as were almost all professional lookalikes, to arrive one hour later than the time previously arranged with the agency by the client; for that authentic celebrity experience.

It was some sort of corporate social event for some bullshit company. They had a Greek name that probably bore no relation to what the company actually did. The organiser, a tall man with a shaved head and a flamboyant fashion sense was greeting people at the door. His bright yellow shirt stung Sam's eyes worse than the cigarette Sam had resting between his lips.

'OMG,' the organiser said, taking hold of Sea-mouse's hand. 'You look just like him.'

The organizer handed Sea-mouse and Sam a glass of champagne, offered them a canapé, and then gave them both a copy of the company brochure featuring all their latest news. He took out a brown envelope from his pocket containing Sea-mouse's cheque and handed it to him before waving over to a young woman with dyed red hair.

'OMG,' she cooed, 'that's just sooo spooky, you look just like him.'

There were a couple of other look a likes mingling around the party, chattering away with false smiles to all the faceless suits.

Sea-mouse set to work on the room, making sure they got their money's worth by chatting to everyone and acting smooth. For Sea-mouse, acting smooth involved mime shooting people when he spoke to them as if his hands were guns. They weren't guns.

Sam went and got a beer from the bar, he then headed to the buffet to line his stomach with smoked salmon pâté before making a heroic attack on the cheeseboard. A waiter stalked by and offered Sam another glass of champagne, which he slugged down between bites of a blini.

Sam soon tired of the buffet and of all the dirty looks he was receiving from people with a genuine right to sample the spinach roulade. He decided that his time would be better spent sitting at the bar and strolled over to order more drinks for himself and Seamouse, who was bound to be feeling a bit parched after all that socialising.

The lone barman was busy, mixing cocktails for one of the most immaculately dressed women Sam had ever seen. Sam couldn't help staring, she was beautiful, everything about her was perfect; her jet-black hair which some stylist must have spent hours sculpting this morning to complement the lines of her skull, her light violet dress which fitted flawlessly. It was as if she was born to wear that dress. Sam couldn't picture her wearing anything else.

Resting on the bar with his elbow, Sam clocked the woman's name badge, 'Elizabeth.' 'So, what's your name?' he said coyly, staring at the badge, hoping she would warm to him if he made a little joke. He gave her a cool look and then a quick smile, hoping to show her he was interested but not really that bothered. Elizabeth looked Sam up and down, her face scrunching up in repulsion as her eyes fell on Sam's crotch, although clearly, she was trying to hide it out of politeness. Her eyes fell again on Sam's crotch and she shuddered in disgust. She grabbed her pink cocktails as quick as she could before scurrying off to her group of friends. Sam looked down at his lap. There was a big white stain around his fly where he had dribbled toothpaste earlier. He shook his head at Elizabeth and her friends, who were now all sneaking glances at him, whispering things to each other and giggling. Sam was a little annoyed with her reaction more than anything else. She had obviously jumped to all sorts wrong and indecent conclusions about him. It didn't even look like spunk, it could have been sick or anything.

Sam perched himself on a barstool and was sipping daintily at another glass of champagne when one of the look-a-likes swaggered up to the bar with two women, one draped on each arm. Sam presumed that they were look-alikes too, although they could well have been sex workers.

Sam went to order another drink but the look-a-like was already way ahead of him.

'Don't worry about that pal,' the look-a-like said smugly, 'I'll take care of that.' One of the women tongued his ear as if she was real impressed by how frivolous he was with his Hollywood budget.

Sam stared at him. He couldn't help thinking that this guy was good; not only was he behaving like a complete prick, but he actually looked almost identical to Vince. It was uncanny.

'Ummm…' Sam said, still marvelling at the look-alike's similarity to Vince. 'It's a free bar.'

'No, it's alright kid,' Vince said, 'don't worry about it, this round is on me.' His generosity seemed to really impress the girls. They began cupping his balls, taking one each in their hands and smiling, before flicking their tongues into his ears.

'Bottle of your finest champagne, buddy, and whatever he's having,' Vince told the barman.

The barman, who was under strict instructions from the management, opened a bottle of their finest cava.

'You know, it's just spooky,' Sam blurted out at Vince, who was busy stroking the arse of one of the girls, not really paying much attention to Sam. 'You must get this a lot, but seriously, you look just like him.'

Vince raised an eyebrow before swigging the fizzy wine and pouring it into the mouths of the two girls. Much of it dribbling down their chins in lines of froth.

'I sort of work for him you see,' Sam continued, still not bothered that no one was paying much attention to him. 'Well, I work for these guys who work for Vincent Lee, and it's just spooky. You look just like him. I swear to God, you must be the best lookalike in this place.'

Vince looked at Sam. 'Girls, take a hike,' he ordered, pointing away from the bar with his thumb, his mood changing dramatically. The two women swanned off, but they weren't happy about it. In fact, they seemed rather aggrieved.

Vince sidled up to Sam and slung his arm around him. 'Hey kid,' Vince said, 'I know who you are.'

Sam was a little confused, he had been to several of these types of parties with Sea-mouse, but he couldn't remember ever meeting a Vince look-alike before. He thought that he would definitely remember meeting a look-alike as good as this one. 'Um, sorry, have we met?'

'Not as such,' Vince said in such a smarmy way that it was quite disconcerting for Sam. 'You kind of work for me. You're that schmuck that freakshow Tony hired.'

Sam stared at Vince.

'Yeah, that's right buddy,' Vince said, grinning knowingly.

'So, you really are…?'

'Yep, I really am,' Vince said, still grinning. 'Pretty good racket, ain't it?'

'But you don't need the cash.'

'I don't go signing with look-alike agencies around the world for the cash, I'm Vincent Lee.' Vince seemed quite annoyed at Sam's insinuation. 'I do it for the action right, the partying, the pussy.' Vince topped his glass up. 'Everyone thinks I'm a dumbass lookalike.'

'Well, I suppose it makes sense,' Sam said.

'Too fucking right it does. No one in the world believes I am really me. Not the paparazzi, not no one. I can get as fucked as I want to, roll out of here at three in the morning sticking my fingers up as many skirts as I please and it's not going to appear in tomorrow's papers.'

All Sam could think was 'what a prick', but he still nodded and smiled at Vince as if it was the greatest idea he had ever heard.

Vince, who did actually think that it probably was the greatest idea Sam had ever heard, raised his glass. 'I could get into a fight if I wanted to,' he added, downing the glass in one.

'Right,' Sam said.

Vince topped his glass up from the bottle again before flicking a cigarette up in the air and catching it in his mouth in such a clearly over-practiced manoeuvre to be able to consider it cool. 'So…' Vince said, 'I hear you were the one who did that little job for David Morgan OBE's mother.'

Vince began laughing in an evil, throaty haw-haw sort of way. Sam didn't, he stared blankly at Vince, trying to erase that whole episode from his mind.

'Man, I wish I could have been there. I bet the look on her face was priceless.'

'She was certainly quite distressed,' Sam said.

'I bet she was. Man, I wish I could have seen the look on her stupid face as she realised how vindictive it was. I should have got you to film it, I really should have.'

Sam's fist was clenched tight, he was putting some serious consideration into punching Vince in the face.

'I should have gotten you to video David Morgan OBE too, when he found out about what had happened. I bet the look on that fucker's face was priceless too.'

Sam tried to concentrate on his drink.

'I should have had you all wired up to film the look on Mrs. Morgan's face, and then sent that tape to David Morgan OBE, and got you to film the look on his face as he watched the look on her face.'

Sam couldn't help noticing out of the corner of his eye that Vince was starting to get an erection, his expensive made to measure suit trousers no longer fitting perfectly at the crotch. Sam spun around away from the bar, away from Vince's hard on. Vince, who was out of his trance now, had gotten bored of talking to Sam. He finished his drink, tucked his erection into the elastic of his underpants, and then headed off towards the dance floor to try and find some more skirt.

#

At the other end of the club, by the entrance, a man who had turned up uninvited claiming to be a photographer hired for the event, took a couple more photos before sneaking back out the front door.

Chapter Eleven

Sexfiend roared up to the curb in his brand-new BMW, bought only hours earlier. He slammed on his computer assisted brakes, which worked even more efficiently than he had expected, although still not well enough as he cracked into the rear of the piece of shit some idiot had parked in front of him. The piece of shit in front of him was a Beemer too, but a slightly older model. Sexfiend's tastelessly over the top alloys scratched against the rugged concrete of the curb, making a terrible din. He wrenched the handbrake up, turned the ignition off, and got out of the car, slamming the door after him with both hands. Without even bothering to survey the damage he had done to either his car or the one it was embedded into, he stomped down the street to David Morgan OBE's place.

As the casual observer might have noticed, while out walking their dog or something, Sexfiend was in a foul mood. He had paid two women to lick his arsehole clean that morning, but still he was in the most fearsome of tempers.

In the grand scheme of things, Sexfiend had gotten off pretty lightly from Vince's grand scheme of things. Sexfiend's family were already dead, apart from a few stragglers who had already disowned him. His friends and loved ones, if you could call them that, were well aware of his deviant behaviour. This wasn't the result of Vince's investigations, nor was it the rumour mill at work among Sexfiend's social group. It all came straight from the horse's mouth. Sexfiend told everyone he knew, and even people he had only just met, all about his sexual misadventures dating back to his first erection. It was something he was proud of.

Quite frankly, Vince had bigger fish to fry. As rich as he was, wasting money exposing Sexfiend to the general public just didn't seem worthwhile. Ironically enough, Sexfiend could often be found exposing himself to the general public.

Instead of any major smear campaign, Sexfiend had gotten away with a couple of late-night TV adverts; one detailing his penchant for golden showers, including some strategically blurred stills from his homemade porn, which Sexfiend readily distributed among people he knew. The other showing grainy footage shot by Johnny Cheung of Sexfiend and a colleague stumbling blind drunk out of The Ivy after one particularly long lunch involving some of the finest wines ever to grace man's lips. It also showed him shoving an old couple, who had just been quietly celebrating their 40th wedding anniversary. Sexfiend then threatened to fight them, waving his fists about manically. 'Queensbury rules, you old fuck,' he had shouted at the top of his lungs to the cowering couple, although that hadn't been picked up on the camera's rudimentary microphone system. All this Sexfiend did because he thought it was fun, and so he could steal their taxi, which they had booked in advance and had been patiently waiting for outside the restaurant.

Sexfiend wasn't so much annoyed about the TV adverts, they simply helped him reach his perversions out to a wider audience, which in turn got the exhibitionist in him hard. Extremely hard. No, what reddened Sexfiend's chops, besides autoerotic asphyxiation while he masturbated every morning, was the fact that somebody, some cunt, some fucking cunt, some complete bunch of fucking cunts would have the audacity, the lead weighted balls to attack him. He was furious, mind-bendingly livid that there were people out there who would try something with him. Especially when he could have them killed. Surely, they must know that? Out of all the people Sexfiend had threatened to have killed, he would have given them all up just to threaten these cunts who had done this to him.

#

Sexfiend stepped up to David Morgan OBE's front door, scratched himself through the pocket of his trousers for an obscenely extended period of time, sniffed his hand, and then rang the doorbell.

After a few moments, a middle-aged woman, dressed like a 19th century maid and with a solemn look, who had in fact been hired through an agency specialising in domestic staff with 19th century values, opened the door. 'Mr. David is waiting for you,' she said through facial expression alone, leading Sexfiend inside.

Sexfiend had been to David Morgan OBE's place many times before, but every time he came, he couldn't help being struck by how old fashioned, how Victorian the interior had been designed. It was straight out of a Sherlock Holmes novel. It seemed like not a single furnishing had been made after the Boer war, which taken as a whole, made the styling seem kind of modern. like a lifestyle choice, which is what it was.

The maid showed Sexfiend down the hallway and into the large study where David Morgan OBE was waiting, before she vanished without hardly being noticed.

David Morgan OBE was leaning against the large, extravagant fireplace, drinking brandy from a bulbous crystal brandy glass. There were bookshelves against each wall, each and every one of them packed full of antiquarian books, read many times over the decades but none of them by David Morgan OBE. A large grandfather clock with some fine walnut side panelling was tick-tock, tick-tocking heavily beside the doorway, slower than time. About the fireplace were four leather armchairs. Ricky Belane was sat in one of them, sipping at a glass of brandy nervously, feeling an air of foreboding emanate from the gas lamps around the ceiling, and from Sexfiend's glower, which was almost as sinister as the smug, calculating look David Morgan OBE was sporting.

'Take a seat,' David Morgan OBE said coolly, with a knowing look. As if he had been planning on saying that to Sexfiend for a while, which he had.

'So, have you got to the bottom of all this shit?' Sexfiend asked, as he dropped himself onto a chair as hard as he could, the sudden impact of his sturdy frame causing the room to shake.

'Maybe,' David Morgan OBE said, taking a glass from the tray his newly reappeared maid was holding. She dutifully offered a drink each to Sexfiend and Ricky Belane, and then, she dutifully got down on her hands and knees and crawled out of the room, vanishing again without anyone really noticing she had been there at all.

David Morgan OBE placed his brandy on the mantelpiece and picked up a large brown envelope. He took out some photographs and flicked them on to Sexfiend's lap. 'Do you recognise the man in these?' he asked.

Sexfiend thumbed through a few, briefly glancing at them until he finally fixed his glower onto a picture of Sam spilling a vol-au-vent down his shirt. 'Of course I recognise him,' he finally said, looking up at David Morgan OBE. 'The prick used to work for me until I sacked him a couple of weeks ago. He's a waste of space.'

'Quite,' David Morgan OBE said smugly, tapping his fingertips together in the universal hand gesture of a prat. 'Our man Belane here believes that this is who took those pictures of him.'

Ricky Belane grimaced at Sexfiend sheepishly.

'What, and you think he's doing all this as some sort of vendetta against the media?'

'It crossed my mind, but no. From what I know of this man, he's a lazy, good for nothing. Do you really think he would have the wherewithal, or could even be bothered to plan and execute something like this?'

Sexfiend shook his head. If he had the slightest inkling that Sam was capable of something this seedy, he would have made him an executive long ago. 'So why is he doing this?'

'I followed him to a private detective agency which I believe he is working for,' Ricky Belane chipped in.

'So, who hired them?' Sexfiend asked, just wishing that David Morgan OBE would get to the point.

'Well,' David Morgan OBE said, swilling his brandy around for dramatic effect. 'I'm not sure yet.'

'Brilliant,' Sexfiend said.

'It won't take us long to get to the bottom of this conspiracy,' David Morgan OBE continued. He took another photograph out of the envelope and handed it to Sexfiend. 'There is this though.'

'Is that who I think it is?' Sexfiend asked almost the instant he looked at the photo.

'That's the thing,' Ricky Belane piped up, forgetting himself, 'the party where I took those pictures was full of lookalikes.'

'If you're quite finished,' David Morgan OBE said sharply, slapping Ricky Belane around the face.

'I've seen a lot of look-alikes in my time,' Sexfiend said, 'even used a couple myself on the network, but never have they looked like someone famous before.

David Morgan OBE said, 'I've put that moron on my front page so many times that I'd recognise him anywhere, but we need to be sure before we approach him.'

'Why?' Sexfiend asked.

'Because otherwise we're just wasting our fucking time,' David Morgan OBE shouted.

'OK, fine,' Sexfiend said gingerly. 'So while you're looking into this actor prick, what are we going to do about this other prick?' Sexfiend held up the photo of Sam and waved it at David Morgan OBE.

'He has to pay,' Ricky Belane said with an acidic tongue, spitting up bile with his words. David Morgan OBE and Sexfiend stared at him again, wondering why he kept thinking he had the right to speak.

'The kid is correct though,' Sexfiend admitted. 'He does have to pay. I could have that son-of-a-bitch killed.'

'A tempting prospect, but no. I've got something far better in mind,' David Morgan OBE said with an evil glint in his eye, throwing the remains of his brandy into the fire, making the flames pounce, for dramatic effect.

'Better than having him killed?' Sexfiend grumbled. He really wanted to have Sam killed. He wanted to have him killed a couple of weeks ago when he had sacked him. But now, he really really wanted to have him killed. It seemed like the next logical step.

'What are you going to do then, buy him a fucking present,' Sexfiend said, his pathetic wit mustering up its reserves of strength and allowing him slightly more sarcasm than his last effort.

David Morgan OBE pondered this with a bemused smirk on his face, for dramatic effect. 'In a manner of speaking,' he finally said, still with the bemused smirk on his face, for even more dramatic effect.

Sexfiend gave David Morgan OBE a what-the-fuck look, which meant his face scrunched up, kind of like a cunt. Ricky Belane gave him a what-the-fuck look too, but no one noticed because he really wasn't important.

David Morgan OBE strolled over to one of his bookshelves at the far end of the room. He ran his hand along a row of dusty old books, finally bringing it to rest on an early edition of Don Quixote which he then tilted back forty-five degrees, although slyly with his other hand he was pressing a secret button hidden on the underside of the shelf. The whole wall swung inwards smoothly, revealing a brand-new room to his guests, which was almost as big as the one they were sitting in.

'Gentleman, this way,' David Morgan OBE said, entering the hidden room. The other two got up and followed. What they found were dozens of large glass cabinets, each one full with meticulously placed swords of various styles, eras and origin. There were short swords, long swords, broad swords, daggers, sabres, foils, cutlasses, even a few bayonets, and there was a whole massive cabinet dedicated to Japanese swords. Inexplicably, the maid had appeared, standing in front of a suit of armour brandishing another tray of drinks. Everyone gladly took up a fresh glass, although in a slightly baffled way, and no one could remember her leaving.

'Gentleman, this is my collection,' David Morgan OBE said proudly with a glazed look in his eyes.

Sexfiend was shocked. He thought he knew David Morgan OBE, but after all these years he had never realised that he was such a psychopath. He wished he had known a lot sooner because he thought it was really cool. Ricky Belane just hoped that nothing in the room was going to be used on him.

'This has taken me nearly a lifetime to acquire,' David Morgan OBE said, spinning round slowly with his hands outstretched, as if he were a super villain in a film.

'How much did this little lot set you back?' Sexfiend asked, always impressed by gratuitous overspending. That and shiny things, and a lot of these weapons sure were shiny.

'Well,' David Morgan OBE said, pretending to be slightly embarrassed, 'let's just say a lot.'

Ricky Belane stroked a suit of armour, retreating quickly as it began to rattle.

'These aren't just swords,' David Morgan OBE said, 'they're genuine antiques, each one tells a story. Some of them are over a thousand years old, and they've all been used.'

'What, so these have all been used to kill someone,' Sexfiend said, starting to get quite interested now.

'Sure, they've all got to have a death count, otherwise what is the point?'

Sexfiend nodded in agreement, looking around in a new-found admiration for the swords, imagining all of the possible things they had been used to do.

'This one though,' David Morgan OBE said, opening one of the glass cabinets and picking up a particularly elegant double-edged rapier with a masterfully crafted cup-hilt, emblazoned with figures from Greek mythology. 'This one is probably my favourite, although it's certainly not the most expensive.' He rubbed his thumb against the blade, testing its sharpness, even though he already knew that it was finer than any razor ever could be. He smiled fondly at the sword before beginning his story. 'In the 16th century, a Lord was murdered by his brother who then took control of the family estate.' David Morgan

OBE tested the weight of his beloved sword in his hand, bobbing it up and down. He whipped it through the air a couple of times dangerously close to Ricky Belane, who winced with every swish.

'The Lord's son, who was only a small boy at the time, swore revenge. He took his father's sword and hid it from his uncle. Then, when he was thirteen, he'd grown a full bush of pubes and decided that he was now a man. He retrieved the sword from its hiding place and snuck over to one of the house's lavatories, concealing himself in the sewage pit. Back then of course they didn't really have any proper plumbing to speak of, just sort of a wooden bench with a hole in the middle which emptied into a large pit in the ground. A large, shitty pit. There were several of these kinds of toilets about the lower quarters of the house, so there was no guarantee that his uncle would use that particular one for some time, but there he waited, and waited. He waited in that foul-smelling foulness for nearly two days. He hadn't eaten, for obvious reasons. He was weak, he was dehydrated, and he was starting to hallucinate, but still he waited, not making a sound even though a whole stream of people were popping in and out to use the facilities, pissing and shitting on top of him. Finally, after all that time, his endurance paid off. He heard his uncle's voice faintly, laughing and joking, getting closer and closer. Then, eventually, he caught a glimpse of his uncle, the man who had slaughtered his father, as he looked up through the hole in the bench. He waited still, even though the suspense was nearly killing him. His heart was pounding faster and faster and his quarry was getting closer. He took hold of his father's sword with both hands, gripping it tight. His uncle's bare buttocks came into view, blocking out what little light there was in the pit as he sat down. Just as a large lump of his uncle's turd landed on his shoulder, he drove his father's sword up through his uncle's expanding anus, twisting it violently as the tip pierced his heart, killing him almost instantly. The boy left the sword where it was, still stuck to the hilt in human guts. He made his escape out the cleaning tunnels and eventually, some years later, he regained control of the family fortune.' David Morgan OBE paused, for dramatic effect.

'This, gentlemen,' he finally said, testing the edge of the sword again with his thumb, 'is that very sword, removed from the man's anus.' David Morgan OBE was smiling proudly, expecting everyone to be as impressed with this as he was. Ricky Belane stepped back a pace, as disgusted as a child would be if offered a sprout. Sexfiend stood his ground. He was eying the blade with ever increasing interest, trying to see if he could spot any remnants of centuries old faeces, or maybe even some blood.

'Is this the sort of thing you had in mind for those pricks?' Sexfiend asked, rubbing his grubby mitts together. Sexfiend's mitts would always be grubby, no matter how much he washed them.

'Not quite,' David Morgan OBE said. 'I have something far better planned. Let's just say that by this time tomorrow, our young former journalist is going to be a young former breathing person.' With this, he began to laugh. Not a particularly evil laugh which was what he was trying for. It was just slightly irritating with a hint of malice.

'Excellent,' Sexfiend said, 'and you're sure that this plan won't fail?'

'Certainly not. I've already set things in motion,' David Morgan OBE said, making a mental note to set things in motion as soon as everyone had left.

'Good enough for me,' Sexfiend said cheerfully, swiping up another brandy from the maid who had suddenly appeared out of nowhere again. He was blissfully aware that he was starting to feel the alcohol take hold and he still had to drive home. 'Let's toast an end to all this bullshit then with a few more of these,' he said, holding up his glass.

'To new endings,' David Morgan OBE said confidently, clinking his glass with Sexfiend's.

'New endings,' Ricky Belane mumbled, lightly tapping his glass against the others.

Chapter Twelve

Sam straightened his cheap tie in front of the mirror, before awkwardly undoing it, lengthening the fat end and trying again. Sam could tie a tie, he had to wear one of the pointless things every day at the newsroom. He just hadn't done it for a while and there was still a lot of booze in his system, and a whole lot more that wanted to be in there. It's not as if he even had to wear a tie for work anymore. Tony and Johnny Cheung both dressed pretty sharp, but that was just their style. They didn't really care what Sam wore on the job so long as he was reasonably presentable. Most of the time Sam was fine with just a shirt and ill-fitting trousers, sometimes a jacket. Today was different. Sam had decided to turn over a new leaf, take some of Ford's advice; accept what you've got to do, knuckle down, and do it the best you can with all the energy and enthusiasm you can muster. The tie was just the first step. He was going to settle down. Try and stick with this job, maybe even shine a little.

At least he liked working with Tony and Johnny Cheung, they were good guys really, once you got to know them. Sam figured that as soon as this case wound down things would get better. The next case was bound to be more palatable. Reuniting a runaway child with worried parents or helping environmental groups nail greedy companies illegally dumping toxic waste. Vince couldn't keep his crusade going forever. As rich as he was, this was costing a lot of money and sooner or later, he must get tired of it. Then there were the inevitable repercussions to all of this. Of that fact, Sam had no doubt. The media helped shape Vincent Lee into the phenomenon he was today, and they could sure as fuck help to ruin him. Vince wasn't a particularly talented actor. He wasn't bad, he could cry fairly convincingly on cue. Somewhat of a requirement when you cheated on so many girlfriends. But he did need there to be a certain buzz about his private life, otherwise the box office draw wouldn't be so good. Then he'd stop getting all the decent parts and slowly, but surely, his celebrity would ebb away. A vicious circle of failure.

Sam straightened his tie again before he was finally satisfied. He picked off some stray shaving foam from his earlobe and flicked it into the sink.

He checked his watch, still an hour to go until he had to catch his bus. He went into the kitchen and made himself a piece of toast. The kettle was still hot so Sam made another cup of tea.

Just as he was gagging on the first sip of his tea, the phone began to ring. Ring, ring. Normally, Sam would have left it for the machine to pick up. Not today however. He was turning over a new leaf. Even the greatest journey must begin with the smallest of steps, as Sam had read off the back of a packet of cigarette papers. He didn't know why it had been printed there. No one did. Not even the marketing people responsible for that packet of cigarette papers, they just had a strong feeling that people who used their papers would insist on something profound to go along with them.

'Hello,' Sam croaked as he picked up the phone, sitting himself down on the sofa.

'Hi darling,' Jane cooed cheerfully down the other end.

'Unnh.' Sam groaned in response. It was too early in the morning for Sam to deal with this.

'Don't be like that,' Jane said, sounding genuinely hurt.

'Well how do you expect me to be after catching you trying to turn me into John Holmes?'

'I know, I know, but that's why I phoned. After the last time I saw you, I've been feeling really bad. I just wanted to call and say I'm sorry.'

'Really?'

'Sure, I would have done this sooner, but I thought I should give you some time to cool down.'

Sam remained silent, taking another sip of tea and wondering if he could trust her.

'Yeah,' Jane continued, 'I was just lying here in bed, thinking of you and how I've been bothering you so much. I just thought that I should get on and apologise. For everything. I don't know what came over me.'

'That's okay,' Sam said, feeling bad for the way he had reacted to her advances. 'We're still friends and everything. I just don't want to be in porn. You don't have to go getting yourself all upset.'

'I know. But I was just lying here, wearing one of your old Thin Lizzy T-shirts, thinking of you.'

'You still wear my old T-shirts?'

'Oh yes,' Jane cooed, 'I always sleep in your T-shirts, they're strangely comforting. Your T-shirts and a nice, tight pair of panties.'

Sam's suspicions were aroused, as well as his penis. He would be a fool not to be suspicious with Jane talking like this again. He couldn't help himself though, from imagining Jane lying there in bed, her panties riding up her crack. He wanted to be there with her, like it used to be when he would wake up in the morning, legs and crotches mangled together like a badly tied knot. He wanted to be able to smell her and be able to feel her touch. Slowly, as if he were on automatic pilot, Sam's hand began to work its way down his trousers and into his underpants. 'Are you taping this?' Sam suddenly blurted out, once again aware that he could well be appearing in some sort of phone sex porn, although God knows who it would be marketed for.

'No,' Jane responded innocently, licking her finger before sliding it down between her legs. 'Are you touching yourself?' she asked.

'Maybe,' Sam said, having now unzipped his trousers and pulling them down past his thighs, starting to go at it full blast.

'Good, because I am.'

Sam heard the click of a tape recorder being switched on but he no longer cared. No one would be able to see his face, he'd checked the house for cameras with his evotech401debugger only a few days ago. It was only his voice and his groans, who cared about people listening to that as they jacked off. He just pumped his cock with a good, gentle, medium paced, early morning rhythm.

'Mmmh, I've got a couple of fingers up there now,' Jane groaned seductively, her voice full of sex, like a cheap hotel. 'I bet you'd like to lick them when I pull them out. Tell me you'd like to lick them.'

'Nngh, that would be good,' Sam gasped.

'Oooh, I'm close,' Jane said, almost forgetting that she was talking to Sam down the phone, imagining that he was right there with her as her chuff began to feel like it was literally going to explode.

Suddenly, as if it were timed for maximum inconvenience, there was a knock at Sam's door. He tried to ignore it, for obvious reasons, but it just became a lot more aggressive, as if someone were trying to kick the whole fucking door in, wall and all. It was putting Sam off his stroke, leaving him in somewhat of a quandary. Should he try and finish himself off and then go get the door, or stop half cocked, compose himself, and get the door as soon as possible, in case it was important? It sure sounded important. Sam took the only option he saw available to him. He gritted his teeth and went at it as frantically as possible, his hand a blur, sweat dripping from his now very red, almost purple face. The banging increased in vigour. It was taking all of the enjoyment out of the experience, although Sam was determined to work through it.

Jane could hear his grunting, completely unaware of how soon she was going to lose him. Sam reached down to the floor with his free hand, groping around for a discarded sock, which he knew would be around there somewhere. He finally hooked it up with his fingers, just in the nick of time.

'Oooh, tell me what you'd like to do to me,' Jane said, almost whispering. She was attempting to switch on the camcorder pointed at her bed with her big toe, so she could capture herself in the final throes of ecstasy for the whole world to see, so long as they had a valid credit card.

It was too late.

'I'll call you back,' Sam said as he ejaculated quite a considerable amount into the fabric of his dirty old sock. 'I've got to go!'

'Bastard,' Jane screamed down the other end, taking Sam's ear off. 'I haven't finished yet. Now tell me what you'd like to do to me.'

There was a punch at Sam's door, then a fearsome kick followed by another quick punch.

'Sorry,' Sam said apologetically, 'I'll call you back, I promise,' hanging up the phone before he could be subjected to her response. He pulled the sock off of his penis, which had already gone floppy, and threw the sodden thing on the floor.

Sam stood up, got his clothes back on properly and in order. He stuck his hands in his trouser pockets to wipe them off a bit. He intended to wash his hands as soon as was convenient. After all, he wasn't a pervert. Sam then waddled off to get the door, half hunched with his backside protruding out so that he could rearrange himself as he moved.

Sam quickly wiped his wanking hand again on the wall before opening the front door.

The delivery man dropped a rather battered parcel at Sam's feet, just as he was reaching to take it. The delivery man then held a clipboard irritatingly close to Sam's face and jiggled it about a bit.

'Sign here,' he said, sounding incredibly bored, as if he didn't much care whether Sam signed the thing or not.

Sam bent down and picked up the sorry looking package, his knees creaked with a mild twinge of pain shooting through his legs. Something which had been happening more in recent years.

The battered and bruised brown cardboard box didn't really weigh very much. There was definitely something quite solid in there though, Sam thought to himself as he shook and rattled it about. He balanced the box on his knees and ripped off the brown packaging tape. Inside he could see what looked like the blade of a knife. He carefully pulled it out, spilling most of the vomit yellow crisps of packing foam on the floor. It looked Japanese, like a miniature samurai sword. The blade was about a foot long and had been immaculately polished. Sam could see his reflection in it. He gripped the handle and stabbed it into the air playfully, like he imagined an assassin might, gutting a victim in one artful stroke. It felt cool, made him feel powerful even though he was only mucking about. Another curious look inside the box and he revealed a note which he quickly retrieved. He hoped that it might explain things a bit better, assuming that it must have been sent to him by mistake. The note did explain things a bit better, but he still wasn't sure that he understood. All there was on the carefully folded piece of writing paper, the expensive kind, was a badly drawn stick man who appeared to be either kneeling down or sat cross legged. Whoever had drawn it had no artistic talent whatsoever. The stick man was definitely stabbing himself in the abdomen, there was no mistaking that aspect. There were gory spurts of blood coming out of the poor stickman, shakily drawn in red biro. The person who had done this had obviously put a fair bit of time and effort into it. Also, with the same hand that had written the address, the message 'you know what to do!!!' could be found underneath the picture. Sam didn't really know what he was supposed to do, but he was unnerved. There was definitely some malice locked up in this cryptic message. Either the sender wanted Sam to stab himself in the abdomen, or someone who was kneeling down. Sam felt sure that he wasn't going to do either. He couldn't help thinking that his life had been becoming more complicated in recent weeks.

Sam folded the note up and tucked it into his pocket. He placed the knife on the sofa. He looked at it for a couple of seconds, worrying that he could come home drunk and completely forget all about it, savagely slashing himself in the buttocks as he slumped himself down. He quickly grabbed the knife, took it into the kitchen and stuffed it into the drawer with all the cutlery, finally satisfied that it could do no harm.

#

Sam was late when he finally stepped into the office. No one seemed to notice or care. Johnny Cheung was sat at his desk making an odd gurgling noise as he sucked at his lunchbox sized carton of fruit juice through an elaborate curly straw. Tony was making himself busy watering the plants with a dainty little watering can which looked ridiculous in his large, hamlike hands.

'Sorry I'm late,' Sam said..

'Not to cunting worry m'lad,' Tony said as he carefully wiped down the leaves of his favourite rubber plant with a damp cloth. 'We're taking things slowly today.'

'Something strange happened to me this morning,' Sam told Tony, interrupted momentarily as Johnny Cheung placed his spent juice carton on his desk and gave it a determined thump, producing a loud bang and spray of juice across the room. 'Well, something strange got sent to me this morning,' Sam continued uneasily, starting to feel rather foolish. 'I've been thinking about it on the way here and I think I've worked out what it means.'

Tony stopped what he was doing and gave Sam a curious look. 'For cunt's sake man, spit it out,' he said, stroking his plant idly.

'Was it a knife?' Johnny Cheung asked, his head resting in his arms.

'Um, yes,' Sam said a bit taken aback.

'Aaah,' Tony said dismissively, 'we both got one of those cunts this morning,' he waved a hand over towards the other end of the room before getting back to the important business of his plants. Sam looked over to where Tony had pointed. A knife, identical to the one he had was stuck firmly up to the hilt in a hapless filing cabinet.

'I bet Tony he couldn't hit that picture from over here,' Johnny Cheung said as way of explanation.

'Did they come with a note?' Sam enquired. Johnny Cheung nodded into his arms which Sam took to mean yes. Thinking about it, he wasn't really surprised that Tony and Johnny Cheung had been sent the same thing, it just went towards supporting his theory.

'I think I know who sent this crap,' Sam said proudly, expecting one of those hushed silences of nervous anticipation.

'Yeah, it was that cunt David Morgan,' Tony said, not even bothering to turn round from his plant.

'Oh,' Sam said, unable to hide his disappointment. 'How did you find out?' Again, only a few minutes into the working day, Sam felt slightly foolish in front of his work colleagues. These were, after all, professional detectives and surveillance specialists. They could have found out through their network of contacts, or by hacking into the delivery company's computer system.

'We chased down the delivery driver,' Johnny Cheung said. 'Tony grabbed him by the balls and threatened to dip them in hot coffee until he gave us the paperwork for those parcels.'

'Old methods are always the best,' Tony said, beaming.

'Well, what are we going to do about it? I think he wants us to kill ourselves or else he'll have it done for us.' Sam didn't want to seem like a wimp, but this was getting serious.

'We aren't going to do a cunting thing about,' Tony said in a triumphant sort of way, his hands planted firmly on his hips, one of them still clutching the dinky little watering can. 'Our first task for today is to get some breakfast,' he said. 'Then we're going to try and film that cunt of a paparazzi having a wank in the cinema. We missed him at it last week, but I'm sure he'll be beating off again this afternoon. Photographers are creatures of habit.'

'And we've got to go through the bins at the newspaper again,' Johnny Cheung added, glancing over at Sam quickly, meaning that it was him who had to rummage around through the slop again.

Sam rearranged his tie. Partly because it was becoming uncomfortable and partly because he wanted someone to notice it and possibly comment favourably. They didn't. 'Okay,' he finally said. 'Sounds like a sensible plan of action.'

'There's m'cunting lad. Put this rubbish about the daggers out of your mind. That cunt David Morgan isn't going to do a damn thing. He's just clutching at straws, trying to scare us in his own demented way. So, he knows it's us who've been dishing the dirt. That's a good thing I say, keep the cunt on his toes, rattle his cunting cage. That's what we're being paid for anyway.'

Johnny Cheung was nodding profusely, in agreement with his old friend.

'I suppose,' Sam said, as they headed out towards the black Merc.

'That cunt David Morgan O, B, cunting E ain't going to touch us. Think of all the bad press he would get if he did. He's a public figurehead.' Again, they all agreed with this statement, even Sam who was desperately trying to forget about the fact that David Morgan OBE and his cronies ran the media. All of it. He could quite easily do whatever the hell he wanted and the public would be none the wiser. He hoped that he wasn't the only one concerned about this. He thought that Johnny Cheung at least would be aware of the potential peril they had put themselves in. Breakfast did sound good though. Sam could do with some of that. Toast and coffee just didn't cut it when you had a sturdy hangover.

#

Vince looked at the delivery boy like he was a big, steaming turd. The brown uniform only added to this impression, although it was Vince who was steaming. Literally steaming, the cool air from outside mixing with his sweat drenched body as he leant against his front door creating a faint mist of water vapor and pheromones.

'You're going to have to sign for that,' the delivery boy said unenthusiastically.

'Sign for it your fucking self,' Vince barked as he slammed the door in his face. He wasn't sure what he was most annoyed about. Being disturbed for a silly package, which Vince had thrown to the floor as soon as he had been handed it, or the fact that the delivery boy had shown no interest whatsoever when confronted by a screen legend, or shown even the hint of astonishment when that screen legend turned out to be stark bollock naked. Vince couldn't figure out what was wrong with the guy.

He headed back to his bedroom. 'Now, back to business,' Vince said to Leela, who was still securely fastened to the bed.

'I can't believe you stopped to get the door,' Leela said.

'Well, it gave us a good little breather so we can start afresh. Come at it from a different angle so to speak.' Leela noticed that Vince had collected his

Oscar from the stand opposite the bed as he crept back to her.

'Oh, not that again,' she whined, tired of this routine and even more unimpressed with him.

'Shut up baby, you love it,' Vince said gruffly, licking his lips in that most vulgar fashion of his, even though he knew how much it irritated her.

'Go on then,' she said, realising that she had to indulge him every once in a while.

Vince would have probably done it anyway. She was tied up, but he was delighted to hear her give him the ok. He gave the head of the weighty, gold-plated statue a quick gob of spit to get it lubricated, before stuffing it firmly into his anus. He held it there with his arm stretched behind his back, moving himself into an incredibly uncomfortable but effective position, one leg bent over hers, the other flailing about towards the floor. He planted his free hand on the mattress by her waist, steadying himself as he began to thrust with both the Oscar and his cock.

'And the Oscar for best actor goes to…' Vince whimpered, all the muscles in his legs beginning to tremble.

Chapter Thirteen

'This will not stand,' David Morgan OBE screamed at Sexfiend. 'This will not stand.'

'I'm sorry,' Sexfiend said as apologetically as he could, staring blankly at his mobile phone as if it might help.

'This just won't stand,' David Morgan OBE reiterated. 'You promised me that you could have them killed. You assured me on numerous occasions.'

'Well normally I can,' he protested, 'but for some reason I can't get hold of my man. He must have gone away or something.'

'Well, it won't stand.'

'What about you?' Sexfiend said, starting to get defensive. It wasn't all his fault after all. 'You said you'd sorted it out. You said that by now, they would all be dead. All of them.'

David Morgan OBE thought about this for a while. They should all be dead by now. He couldn't believe that his plan had failed, it was a perfectly logical plan. Why they couldn't have the decency to commit hara-kiri, David Morgan OBE could not understand. He had felt sure that they would see the error of their lamentable ways and end their lives like men. It showed a total lack of respect.

Sexfiend tried his phone again, shaking his head theatrically to show that he still couldn't get through. He had threatened so many people with the prospect of a hit man over the years. He was rich, he could do whatever the fuck he wanted. So naturally, putting two and two together, Sexfiend had every reason to believe that he really could have someone killed. Though the truth of the matter was of all the thousands of people he had threatened, Sexfiend had never actually bothered to go through with it and have them rubbed out. Not even once. So, when David Morgan OBE had come to him, asking for his personal expertise in sorting this little problem of theirs out, he didn't know what to do. After some quick thinking he just phoned his home number knowing that no one would be in to answer. Admitting that he couldn't help never even crossed his mind.

'Do we really need to have them killed anyway?' Sexfiend said. He was starting to have second thoughts about this whole business. 'It will probably die down of its own accord. Why don't we just go home?'

'Oh, just bring more shame on yourself,' David Morgan OBE said. 'You're in this with me whether you like it or not, especially after the pitiful display you've just put on. And I doubt I need to remind you how many shares I own in your pisspot company.'

'No,' Sexfiend said, kicking his feet.

'And what if I suddenly stopped with the bones I've been throwing you along the way? No more first jump on all my celebrity exclusives. What do you think that would do to your already meagre ratings?'

Sexfiend was outmanoeuvred, which admittedly wasn't hard, but now his hands were really tied. He knew that losing his gossip features would ruin his advertising sales, it was the only thing that people actually wanted to watch.

'Now,' David Morgan OBE said with a sneaky glint in his eye, 'You are going to take me to meet a pimp.'

Sexfiend's ears pricked up and his spirit immediately returned. Now that seemed like a plan he could get behind. He was sorry he had ever doubted his good friend David Morgan OBE.

Chapter Fourteen

Sexfiend had taken David Morgan OBE to see a good pimp. A really great one, who was bound to be able to help. He was six foot four, but with such a slim figure he surely must have a couple of tapeworms floating round his intestine. It was something that had earnt him the nickname of Skin, which was a good pimp nickname, a really great one. Skin always had a fantastic sense of pimp fashion. Today was no exception, wearing as he was, a purple crushed velvet suit and classic bowler hat, all complemented in a pimp sort of a way by the big fat Monte Cristo wedged between his lips.

Sexfiend was sure that Skin would be able to put them onto some good people for sorting out problems, not only because he was aware of Skin's murky criminal past, being completely aroused by that sort of thing, but because Skin was such a damned smooth operator. He was the bees' knees, the cats' whiskers and he could sweet talk the barnacles off of a sperm whale's belly. Just by flashing his gold tooth and unleashing that silver tongue of his, he could make you believe that he could achieve absolutely anything. So, when David Morgan OBE asked Sexfiend to take him to a pimp with contacts, Skin seemed like the obvious choice.

'What makes you boys think lil' ol' Skin can help?' little old Skin said between plumes of cigar smoke, leaning back snugly in the only good pimping chair in the whole sleazy pimp bar, which Skin part owned.

'Well, you're a pimp!' David Morgan OBE said matter of factly.

Skin looked hurt. He always preferred to be referred to as an entertainment manager for one thing, but he also hated people jumping to conclusions. 'Oh, so just because I'm in the b'ness of social relaxation, I go round messing people up and having them whacked willy nilly?'

David Morgan OBE was pretty sure that that was a fairly accurate assumption to make about pimps, he was also fairly sure that Skin was the only pimp ever to use the term willy nilly.

'That's discrimination that is.' Skin said sorely.

'Well, yes, you are a pimp,' David Morgan OBE continued, never being one to spare people's feelings. He was becoming quite frustrated that it was this much trouble just to hire a hitman. 'I mean, what do you do if one of the punters starts playing too rough with one of your girls? Damaging her face or something?'

Skin's pimp brain was deep in pimp calculation. He let out a couple of thick smoke rings and then moved his cigar from one side of his mouth to the other with a well-manicured hand. He was pondering more how much it would cost, cutting the earnings of one of his fine pieces of ass by half.

'Look, I think I can help you guys with what you need,' Skin said, 'but I would be really exposing myself if I provided you with that information. If you boys get caught, I mean.'

Sexfiend was imagining skin, exposing himself, maybe on a bus or the gift shop of a sea life centre. Of course, that wasn't what Skin meant by exposing himself. He was, obviously, talking about the possibility of prosecution, but that also wasn't really what he was talking about. David Morgan OBE understood as he was fully conversant in the universal language of cash. He reached into his trouser pocket and coolly pulled out a fat wad of about one thousand pounds held together by a cheap rubber band. He tossed it into Skin's lap.

'Deal,' Skin said, pocketing the dough. 'You're in luck. The guys who can help you out have been doing a bit of work for me today. They're over there, behind me, playing pool. I gotta tell you though, they don't work for no chump change like what you just gave me.' Skin grinned as he said this, knowing full well that any figure the two knuckleheads behind him could name would be chump change to the joint collateral of Sexfiend and David Morgan OBE, and he was looking at a nice fat slice of the pie as a finder's fee.

\#

'I'll do the talking,' David Morgan OBE whispered to Sexfiend as they made their way over to the abused looking pool table which the hitmen were playing at.

Adrenalin started to kick up a little making them want to either fight or take flight, and it was playing havoc with Sexfiend's brain processes. He was already over stimulated by the excitement of this whole situation and he believed that he would definitely have to get Skin to send a couple of girls round to his place when this last bit of business was finished so that he could calm himself down.

The hitmen were playing pool with all the grace of water buffalo. They were both under the misapprehension that the harder you hit the ball, the better you were at the game.

They weren't exactly the suave and sophisticated but deadly efficient secret agent types David Morgan OBE had always imagined assassins to be. In fact, they were the complete antithesis of that. They looked like a pair of violent, deranged thugs who lacked the brain power to commit anything more than a bit of petty theft and the occasional aggravated assault.

These two stupid, violent, deranged thugs weren't completely brainless, however. Subnormal intellect yes, but not completely brainless, and by a process of natural selection, the competition having all been killed or imprisoned, they had managed to ascend to the top of their game. For example, they had never been idiotic enough to reveal their real names to a client, or even to each other, always being referred to as Mr. Benn and Mr. Ed.

'Erm… can we buy you a drink?' David Morgan OBE said, scratching the back of his head as he tried to work out how to go about this properly.

'Are yous two cops?' the man referred to as Mr. Benn said, walloping the cue ball indiscriminately towards a group of other balls which then proceeded to ricochet off the cushions for so long that statistically speaking, he should have potted something, but he didn't.

The man referred to as Mr. Benn was the larger of the two and consequently the leader. He was a giant of a man with biceps big enough to punch a polar bear in the face and get away with it. His huge beer belly meant that his grubby black t-shirt could no longer be tucked into his grubby stonewash jeans. The man referred to as Mr. Ed, who in his own right was vast, looked like a child in comparison to his partner. His long greasy ponytail and greying beard gave him the look of a roadie for the rock group Status Quo.

'We's don't like cops,' the man referred to as Mr. Ed said, striking the cue ball with equal vigour as his friend and to similar effect.

'Good God no,' David Morgan OBE quickly said, 'We're businessmen, like yourselves. We'd like to offer you a little bit of work if you'd be interested.'

'I heard that you have to tell us if yous are cops,' the man referred to as Mr. Ed said. 'It's the law or something.'

That certainly wasn't the law and if it was, it would have been a stupid law. The man referred to as Mr. Ed was mistaken.

'Skin can vouch for me,' Sexfiend said, hoping that David Morgan OBE wouldn't mind him cutting in.

The two men referred to as Mr. Benn and Mr. Ed glanced over at Skin who was nodding and grinning and waving the bundle of cash about as way of reassurance, which was good enough for these stupid cunts.

The man referred to as Mr. Benn chipped the cue ball off the table and it rocketed towards the bar, smashing through a pint glass and narrowly missing the barman as he dove for cover.

'Shall we call it a draw?' the man referred to as Mr. Benn asked the man referred to as Mr. Ed. He nodded and they both stabbed their cues onto the table. The two thug's games often ended in a draw, usually because they were too bored or drunk to continue, although there had been occasions when the table had become too battered, ripped and cracked to provide any further sport.

'Yous two fucks go and get some beers in,' the man referred to as Mr. Benn said. 'We'll go and get us a table, then we can have a little chat.'

Sexfiend and David Morgan OBE gave each other an anxious look, both thinking that now might be a good time to back out. They were having doubts about these two clowns, even Sexfiend. As untactful as he was, Sexfiend was fairly sure that these bastards didn't know the correct way one went about securing a big contract. From his vast experience in business, the customer was always right. Not in danger of a good old-fashioned beating with a spade or similar blunt instrument. David Morgan OBE and Sexfiend didn't back out however, they just shrugged at each other and then went to the bar.

They weaved their way back, between pimps and knuckleheads, clutching pints of beer in each hand carefully so as not to spill any on their expensive clothes. David Morgan OBE had fancied a white wine spritzer, but he didn't think it was the sort of thing you should have when dealing with the criminal underworld. He thought it might be ok if he asked for it in a dirty glass, but settled for a good old, salt of the earth pint of lager. That was sure to help him fit right in.

They placed the drinks on the table at the corner of the bar and then sat themselves down. The man referred to as Mr. Ed was busy picking shards of pool ball out of his long, greasy hair, along with the odd mummified fly. The man referred to as Mr. Benn took a huge gulp of his beer, then, as a show of strength, took a huge gulp of David Morgan OBE's beer.

'So, what can we do for you?' the man referred to as Mr. Benn said, wiping his lips with his hairy ape like forearm. The man referred to as Mr. Ed flicked what appeared to be a crouton, although it could well have been a piece of fossilized turd, into the ashtray.

'Well, there's a couple of complete fucks who've been messing us about and we want them sorted,' Sexfiend said before David Morgan OBE elbowed him sharply in the ribs.

'There's three fucks… erm… people. Possibly four,' David Morgan OBE stuttered.

'Well, which is it?' The man referred to as Mr. Benn said.

David Morgan OBE considered this. He really wanted to set these two hooligans after Vince as well as the others. He wished it would be as easy to have the prick killed as anyone else. Unfortunately, things didn't always follow the easiest path. Vince was going to be a little more difficult. You just couldn't have a famous movie star murdered without people missing him. The others sure, but not Vince. People would definitely start asking questions. David Morgan OBE decided that he would just have to keep that one on the backburner for a while, try to deal with Vince personally first. He was still hopeful that he would do the decent thing and commit hara-kiri.

'Three,' David Morgan OBE said without conviction. 'Definitely three, the fourth is still under consideration.'

'Right, so we will stick with three for now,' the man referred to as Mr. Benn said. 'What can you tell us about them?'

David Morgan OBE took his handkerchief out of his breast pocket and carefully, so as to not leave fingerprints, used it to pull out an envelope from another pocket which he then placed in front of the two men. 'These are the guys,' he said, 'their photographs and addresses are in there.'

'So what exactly do yous want done to them?' the man referred to as Mr. Ed asked, chewing loudly on a mouthful of peanuts he'd gotten from somewhere, which all the others hoped was a fresh bag of peanuts. 'We have various packages of mindless violence available to suit the needs of even the most modest budgets.'

'Really?' David Morgan OBE asked, surprised by this relatively cogent statement.

'Oh sure, yous got to be versatile in this business. The rules of competition and all that. Simple economic theory.'

'What services do you offer?' Sexfiend asked, purely out of his own prurient interest as they already had their minds set on some killings.

'Well, for fifty quid, Mr. Benn here will kick them all in the nuts a couple of times. Hundred quid will get you the same, plus I'll break their thumbs with a hammer.'

'We were thinking of something a bit more severe than that,' David Morgan OBE said.

Sexfiend nodded gleefully with a hungry look on his face, obviously getting a real kick from all this dirty talk.

'Well, we could always do our special,' the man referred to as Mr. Ed said enthusiastically.

'Special?' David Morgan OBE asked.

'Oh yes, for six grand a piece, we'll beat the piss out of em, drive em out to the middle of nowhere, give em another good kicking, bury em alive for a while, with a bit of hose so's they can breathe, and then we dig em up again the next day,' the man referred to as Mr. Ed explained.

'You bury people alive, then dig them back up again?' David Morgan OBE said, trying to get his head around this concept.

'Oh sure, very popular,' is burying people alive,' the man referred to as Mr. Ed said, getting excited about the prospect of burying someone again. 'Shits em right up.'

The man referred to as Mr. Ed loved burying people alive. Good honest work, getting back to nature, like farming. The man referred to as Mr. Ed was never happier than when he was standing in a hole, up to his neck in dirt, ready to throw some poor sap in and cover the cunt up again.

'Um… No!' David Morgan OBE said, appalled. 'We were thinking of something a little less messy and a lot more permanent.

'No problem,' The man referred to as Mr. Benn said rubbing his hands together. 'We'll just kill 'em.'

'Excellent, that's the ticket,' David Morgan OBE said.

'Won't be cheap though,' the man referred to as Mr. Benn said, licking his lips.

Sexfiend and David Morgan OBE both shrugged indifferently.

'Fifty grand apiece,' the man referred to as Mr. Benn said, licking his lips again.

Sexfiend and David Morgan OBE both shrugged again, indifferently.

'We could bury them just a little bit,' the man referred to as Mr. Ed chipped in sulkily, his arms folded over his chest.

'No! No burying,' David Morgan OBE snapped. 'Just kill them.'

'So, getting back to the hundred and fifty grand,' the man referred to as Mr. Benn said, glowering at his friend.

'No problem,' Sexfiend said. He probably had that much lying about his mansion for prostitutes and other incidentals.

'Yeah, no problem,' David Morgan OBE said getting up, preparing to leave as soon as possible. Unlike Sexfiend, he wasn't used to slumming it. 'We'll have half the cash sent over here in a couple of hours, the second half you'll get when you've got the job done.'

With that, they left, David Morgan OBE picking Sexfiend up and dragging him out by his lapels. No one even thought about shaking hands, so they didn't.

'We could bury them anyway,' the man referred to as Mr. Ed said hopefully to the man referred to as Mr. Benn.

The man referred to as Mr. Benn shook his head. 'Only when they're dead.'

Chapter Fifteen

Tony stretched again, which was quite a feat for such a large man confined to such a small space. The Merc was a luxurious car, inside and out, but after spending so much time within its leather upholstered boundaries, it was becoming somewhat of an ordeal for all three of them. The walls were getting smaller, closing in, and the air conditioning was freeze-drying them alive.

Tony poured himself another cup of coffee from his thermos and drank it down. He picked up his newspaper from his lap and spread it out again ceremoniously on the steering wheel so that he could get back to his crossword. A good crossword was a vital piece of kit for a private investigator engaged in the mind-numbing task of a pointless stakeout.

'Eight across,' Tony said enthusiastically. 'Which cunt's son defeated the Romans at Cannae in 216 BC?'

'Hmm?' Sam mumbled as he stared through his binoculars at David Morgan OBE's office, trying to concentrate on the job in hand to keep his mind off the conditions.

'C'mon, for cunts sake. H, seven something's. His son defeated the cunting Romans at Cannae. What was that cunts name, Hannibal or something?'

'Hamilcar,' Johnny Cheung said idly as he hammered away at his Gameboy, which was another vital piece of kit for a private investigator, involved in the mind-numbing task of a pointless stakeout.

'Excellent, it fits. You're on a cunting roll here JC,' Tony said as he filled in the letters. 'Now, fourteen down: first cunt to reach the peak of Everest?'

'David Morgan's looking at us again,' Sam said, jotting this gem of information down in his notepad. 'He keeps peering at us between the blinds.'

'I think I know this one,' Tony said. 'It was Captain something or other. Had a big moustache.'

'It was Tensing Norgay.'

'Doesn't cunting fit.'

'They're wrong,' Johnny Cheung said, looking up from his Gameboy and shaking his head in disgust at the newspaper. 'Try Edmund Hillary.'

'Yeah, that fits. Was the cunt a captain?'

'I don't see the point of this?' Sam grumbled, unsure of how much more he could take. 'We've been here for over four hours and we haven't seen a thing. We were spotted almost immediately. It's not as if we're actually going to discover anything useful out in the open like this.'

'Yeah, I don't get it either,' Johnny Cheung said. 'We're supposed to be professionals.'

'Look, the fact that we have been spotted is the cunting point,' Tony said half-heartedly. 'As soon as I told him about the dagger, that cunt Vince said that we were going to sit outside this cunt's office so that everyone can see us. It's a show of force or something.' Tony sighed heavily. For the time being, being conspicuous was the name of the game, which made a mockery of the surveillance specialist signs out the front of Tony and Johnny Cheung's office. Vince had insisted on them using a nondescript grey Mondeo, which Tony had flat out refused, although compromises had been made and Tony had installed a huge radio Arial on the roof of the black Merc, making it stick out like a sore thumb. 'I don't get it either, but that cunt was adamant that we do this, and he is paying our wages.' Tony sighed again.

Sam got back to his binoculars. He was still worried about that hara-kiri knife and was more nervous about this new endeavour than the others. 'I just think that this is a bad idea,' Sam muttered to no one in particular.

'I tell you cunting what. Why don't you go and take your lunch break, come back in an hour or so. Me and Johnny here will hold the fort.'

'Really?' Sam said.

'Sure. Why not?' Johnny Cheung said, locking a new cartridge into his Gameboy.

Sam stepped out of the car gasping for breath, the sense of freedom making him feel slightly dizzy; either that or he'd just stood up too quickly. He wondered what he should do now. He had expected that he would have just been sent on a food run and then back to the car to eat stale sandwiches amongst the smell of cheese and onion crisps, even if there were no cheese and onion crisps. That was the normal drill on a stakeout, rather than being released into the real world for a full hour. He spotted the building Ford worked in over the road. Sam figured that he might as well do his good deed for the day and pester Ford at work, see what he was up to, make him feel wanted. He had nothing better to do.

#

'This is great,' Ford said excitedly, stacking some legal files and other paperwork into a neat pile in the middle of his desk. It was oddly comforting for Ford, this little ritual. It was proof that he really got things done around here. It allowed him to tell himself that the whole place would simply grind to a halt if he ever just stopped or wasn't around to do the donkey work.

'We're doing lunch. We never do lunch,' Ford said, leading Sam out of the office. 'Like normal people. Normal working people. And you're almost dressed for business.' Ford was very happy for once. 'We're a couple of associates, about to do lunch.'

On their way out of the offices, Ford stopped at the desk of one of the legal secretaries he'd been trying to impress for some time, which was futile for far too many reasons to list.

'Hold all my calls,' Ford said to the secretary, attempting to sound suave, rather than what he pulled off which was pure asshole. 'Me and my associate are doing lunch.'

She glanced at them momentarily with a total lack of interest and didn't respond, because she had no idea what to do with that information.

Ford's voice wavered, 'and urm… you'd better dig out one of those expense forms for me.'

This did get a reaction, although definitely not the one Ford was fishing for as he tried to impress both her and Sam.

'Are you sure?' she said, belittling him with her smirk.

'We've got to go,' Ford mumbled, deflated. 'Reservations.' He made a show of checking his watch, but you could tell that his spirit wasn't in it.

Sam couldn't help feeling sorry for Ford, who at the end of the day was one of his only friends. It was no wonder that Ford got so worked up all the time, when he had to deal with this sort of shit all day. In an office full of people, Ford passed by a great number with barely even a glance of acknowledgement from any of them, as if he'd only just started there that week, even though he had been there years. A sign of animosity Sam knew only too well from his days as a worker drone. In nature, the rarer the species, the less it is preyed upon. In the world of offices and corporations, the opposite is true. Any sign of difference, of going against the grain, or just not quite fitting in and you are fair game. You are held at a distance, and only brought close to be mocked and belittled, because you didn't read the right magazines or bland literature about coping with relationships, and you didn't aspire to that minimalist flat or deluxe gym membership and had no idea about football. You are just kept far enough away from each of the cliques that you can almost touch them, but not quite, like Tantalus trying to reach for an apple, knee deep in piss water.

Out on the street, Ford led the way towards a coffee bar he'd overheard great things about as he hovered around his colleagues' conversations. They served unpronounceable food and elaborate coffee, at ludicrous prices of course, and you could sit on real bean bags, all of which added up to a classy joint.

'I don't have much time before I've got to be back,' Sam said. 'We're on a stakeout.'

'Don't worry about it, we'll just get a sandwich and double mocha latte.' Ford checked to make sure that he still had his credit card to pay for it. There was no reason to believe that it wouldn't be there, he hadn't been bumped into by any Machiavellian type characters that day. It was just one of Ford's several neuroses, that people were constantly stealing from him. He had to check his possessions whenever the impulse would take him. He couldn't even put his bins out each week without an itching feeling of paranoia that people were rifling through them, after his bank statements.

They had the coffee bar in their sights. They could see it down the street, with its funky glass front and postmodern sign. They quickened their pace, their stomachs starting to rumble and growl at the thought of those grilled Parma ham and buffalo mozzarella paninis.

Sam didn't see the blow coming. If he had, he would have moved out of the way. He hit the floor as if he had died, but he wasn't dead, he wasn't even unconscious, just stunned. His brain appeared to be vibrating inside his skull, and although he could still see, he couldn't really focus on anything. He began to gag on a chunk of tooth, which must have broken off as his face hit the curb.

'Are you sure that was the guy?' The man referred to as Mr. Ed asked.

'Sure it is, look at his picture. It's definitely him.'

Sam received another powerful blow to his testicles, sending waves of excruciating pain up and down his body, and then, the inevitable sickness. Tears began to stream from his eyes as he groaned in agony.

'What did you kick him in the nuts for?' The man referred to as Mr. Benn asked his partner. 'Nobody paid us to kick him in the nuts.'

'What are you, his mother or somethink. I just thought that since those guys shelled out plenty, we should, you know, throw in a few extras. It's the professional thing to do. It's the icing on the cake, the little extras are. The thing they'll be talking about to their friends, saying wonderful things about the service. That sort of word-of-mouth advertising you just can't buy.'

The man referred to as Mr. Benn thought about this for a few moments, then shrugged his shoulders and gave Sam an almighty kick to the testicles himself. At the end of the day, it couldn't hurt to make sure that the victim was fully pacified before transporting him to the car, unless of course you were the victim.

Sam was the victim, and it certainly did hurt. He rolled around on the floor, gasping for breath. He wasn't really scared yet, and he wasn't wondering why these people he couldn't quite see were doing these terrible things to him. He was in too much pain for any of that. Those thought processes were still to come.

'Right, now tape the fucker up and we'll get him in the car,' the man referred to as Mr. Benn said, throwing a roll of gaffer tape into the man referred to as Mr. Ed's hands.

While this beating was going on, Ford did not stand idle. It's a popular misconception that cowards, when attacked, freeze to the spot with fear, too terrified to move, too terrified to think, completely dazed and confused. People who do that are not cowards. They are just plain stupid. Too dumb to move, too dumb to think, too dumb to decide whether to fight or run away. Ford, however, was a coward. As soon as he realised what was happening, that two of the largest brutes he had ever seen in his life were kicking the living shit out of his best and only friend, his fast-thinking lawyer brain calculated that there was absolutely no chance he would be able to help in any sort of physical way. His weedy, narrow, skin and bone frame would have been useless against such bruisers; it would have been suicide. He took the only sensible course of action available to him, which was to flee. And hopefully, when he had finished fleeing, he would be able to find someone who could help.

Ford ran, and ran, and ran. He ran like old people have sex, in short bursts and with the constant fear of a heart attack. He was scared and confused. Sweat was pouring down his face out of exertion and self-loathing, despising himself for not being able to save Sam.

Although it didn't seem like it to him, Ford didn't have to run for very long. By some unlikely stroke of luck, he spotted coming around the corner, the fluorescent jackets and feltish helmets of two police officers, walking the beat. Suddenly, a ray of hope stomping their feet in standard issue shit kicker boots, and still just in sight of the kidnapping in progress. Ford's guts, which had previously started to drop, began to return to normal functioning. His retreat wasn't in vain, the system worked, here were some people who had the training and resources to help.

Ford gasped for breath, pawing at their shiny plastic jackets with his sweaty hands, just trying to make sure that they were real and that they wouldn't go anywhere. 'Help, you've got to help,' he panted. 'My friend… over there.'

'Calm down sir,' one of the officers said in his most patronising voice. 'What seems to be the trouble?'

'Over there,' Ford cried, completely exhausted, pointing urgently towards Sam who could still be seen being beaten badly and dragged along the street by the thugs. 'My friend, look, he's being attacked, you've got to help him.'

The first officer put his hand against his helmet, shielding the sun from his eyes so he could get a good look at all the commotion. 'Ah yes,' he said, 'bit of a ruckus going on down there.'

The second officer had a look too, straining his eyes. 'Oh yeah, I see what you mean. Terrible business,' he said, preparing to move Ford aside and get on his way.

Ford was flabbergasted. 'Terrible business, terrible bloody business. My friend is being savagely attacked and that's all you're going to say, "Terrible business"? Do something, for God's sake.'

The two officers, who were going to let the assault Ford had previously committed slide, stopped in their tracks, horrified at this insolence they were hearing.

'And what do you suppose we do?' the first officer asked.

'What do you mean, what do I suppose you do?' he shouted, 'Arrest them. They're committing a crime, aggravated assault at the very least. Arrest them.'

The second officer didn't particularly appreciate Ford's tone, which he deemed to be disrespectful of his high office and badge. 'Don't you go quoting statistics at me, sonny Jim,' he said calmly, looking down at Ford.

'Every bloody person thinks they know our business,' the first officer said to the second officer, sounding tired. 'Takes years of training to understand the law, sir. You can't just jump in feet first I'm afraid.'

'I know, I'm a lawyer,' Ford yelled out of frustration. 'I know the law, and there's a crime being committed. Now I demand that you both go and arrest the perpetrators before they get away.'

'You're getting very aggressive, sir,' the first officer said with deliberate calm. 'I'm not going to warn you again. Calm down, or I'm afraid I will have to arrest you.'

'Arrest me?' Ford shouted, tearing at his hair. 'Arrest them, look, they're criminals.'

'Right, that's it sir,' the second officer said, his patience having been stretched to its very limit. 'I'm arresting you for assaulting a police officer.'

The two officers looked at each other with puzzled expressions, as if to say, what next?

In a moronic eureka moment, the first officer's eyes lit up, like he knew what to do. He didn't. He swung his police service radio by the cord, around and around his head, eventually bringing it down and twatting Ford in the face, who subsequently dropped to his knees yelling in pain.

The second officer's eyes were zipping left to right and he was mouthing words to himself as he played back his training in his head. 'No, that's not it.' he said, just as Ford was clambering to his feet.

The first officer looked at the second officer for help, but he got nothing but a confused shrug. He decided that now was not the time for indecision and jabbed Ford in the eye with his notebook.

'Aaargh,' Ford yelled, falling back to his knees.

'No, that's still not right is it?' the first officer said.

'Handcuffs!' the second officer said, pointing up towards the sky.

'Oh yeah, that's right, handcuffs,' the first officer said. He grabbed a shiny, nickel-plated pair from his utility belt and swung them round his head a couple of times before bringing them down with all his might onto Fords left kidney.

'Fucking hell,' Ford screamed, his insides feeling like they were about to explode, and not just his bowels this time. 'You put them on my wrists,' he yelped, 'put them on my wrists, just please, stop hitting me.

'Ah, so he admits it,' the second officer said with a satisfied smirk. The first officer nodded sagely as he tried to fit the handcuffs on Ford's bony wrists.

'Look, you can't do this to me,' Ford whimpered, 'I haven't done anything wrong. Arrest them. Please, they're going to kill my best friend.' The tears started to flow out of Ford as the gravity of the situation sunk in. He could barely see Sam now. The two giants had dragged him to a parking bay and were trying to stuff him into the back of a nondescript, grey Mondeo. 'You could still get him back,' Ford cried, 'or at least get the number plate.'

The officers looked at each other and began laughing.

'He's starting to resist arrest now.'

'I'm going to have your badges.' Ford snivelled, making a strange gurgling sound as he cried.

'They don't pay us enough for this shit,' the first officer grumbled, lobbing his battered radio, which bounced off of Ford's temple and clattered down the street, its batteries flying out and rolling into the gutter.

Ford clutched his head with both hands tightly and curled up into a protective ball. He prayed that there wouldn't be a scar where the radio had struck him. He had a meeting tomorrow and golf on Saturday, and he didn't know how he would be able to explain it. There was no way he was going to be able to say he had been arrested, and saying he had an accident would be seen as a sign of weakness. It would be the end of his career before it had even got going.

'You'll have to call this one in,' the first officer said to the second. 'My radio seems to be broken.'

Chapter Sixteen

Sam lay taped up in the back of the car, barely able to move, or breathe. The man referred to as Mr. Ed was sat on his legs, crushing his knees so that they felt like they were starting to bend in directions they were never meant to bend.

Sam's ribs were surely cracked from some overzealous stomping, and his back was burning from where he had been dragged and scraped across the pavement and into the car. The feeling of the cheap fabric of the seats through his ripped clothing and skin was just heightening this agony to new, excruciating levels. This was the worst amount of pain Sam could ever remember experiencing. Every part of his body felt like it was on fire, and thanks to the professional diligence of his captors, he was sure that his balls would never work again.

He had been sick twice now, but due to the tape over his mouth, what didn't dribble out his nose, burning it with butyric acid, he had to swallow back down in forced gulps. He'd read somewhere that once your body had reached a certain level of injury, endorphins were released in such quantity that you no longer felt any pain. Sam felt that he obviously hadn't been hurt that much yet, but it must be close. He began to wonder if the two goons were to beat him just that little bit more, it might help. He didn't really want to stop feeling the pain though. Concentrating on the pain was the only thing keeping him from thinking about what was coming next.

The car ran over a speed bump, at speed, just as Sam was vomiting again, which caught in his throat as his body was jerked about, making him cough and splutter, and convulse and contort as he tried desperately to swallow it back down.

'He's making those funny noises again,' the man referred to as Mr. Ed said, staring curiously at Sam's strange display. 'Do you think we ought to do something?'

'Do something?' the man referred to as Mr. Benn said, turning around in the driver seat to laugh at his partner. 'We're going to kill the cunt, we're not taking him to see his GP, even if he was dying.'

Now Sam wanted those endorphins. Now Sam wanted to feel nothing. He went wild with fear, swearing and cursing which due to his gag, sounded like a series of 'mmphs', and rolling his head from side to side manically. He began trying to wriggle his way out from under the man referred to as Mr. Ed, who was raining blows down on Sam's guts.

Sam knew that at times like this, your whole life was supposed to flash before your eyes, but it wasn't happening. He tried to force it, to dig up some long-forgotten memories, some good times, some bad times even. But he couldn't think. No successes, no regrets. He had nothing. The only thing going through his mind was, oh shit, oh shit, oh shit, oh shit.

'Don't you think we should bury him alive a bit first, you know, and then kill him?' the man referred to as Mr. Ed asked hopefully.

'Oh, for fuck's sake,' the man referred to as Mr. Benn sighed. 'I thought we had sorted that already. We're not burying him at all. We're just going to chuck him in the river.

'The man referred to as Mr. Ed slammed his fist down on Sam's thigh, beginning to sulk again.

The man referred to as Mr. Benn rummaged around in his pockets as he tried to concentrate on the road. 'Shit,' he said, throwing an empty cigarette packet onto the passenger seat. 'You got any smokes Ed?'

'Nope, I smoked the last one while we were following this cunt.'

'Oh man,' the man referred to as Mr. Benn said, 'I'd kill for a cigarette.'

The man referred to as Mr. Ed began to laugh in deep, booming guffaws. He slammed his fist down on Sam's pelvis, chuckling into Sam's face in a very sinister fashion, the sick grin and manic expression giving him the look of something altogether demonic. 'I'd kill for a cigarette,' he laughed, slamming that fist down a couple more times. 'Do you get it?' he asked Sam, 'We kill people, and he said, "I'd kill for a cigarette," you see?'

'So'd I,' Sam said, trying to humanise himself to his captors, although due to the tape on his mouth, it sounded more like 'mmph, mmph'. He was rewarded with a karate chop to the balls, causing Sam to faint from the pain. The man referred to a Mr. Ed prodded him a couple of times to see if he really was out cold. He was kind of upset when Sam didn't respond. It took all the fun out of hurting them when they passed out.

'Oh screw it,' the man referred to as Mr. Benn said. 'There's a garage up here, I'm pulling in to get some tabs.'

The man referred to as Mr. Ed wasn't the quickest of thinkers, but he was quick to note that this probably wasn't the most sensible course of action. 'We do have what looks like a blood-soaked corpse taped up back here,' he said. 'Someone might see him and phone the police.'

'Nah, it's broad daylight. No one ever does shit in broad daylight. They're scared we might see their faces.'

'Even so, they have CCTV all over the place.'

'Relax, it'll be fine. Stick your coat over him if you're worried. I'm gonna stop and get a couple of packs of smokes, and maybe a pasty,' the man referred to as Mr. Benn said.

The man referred to as Mr. Ed was intrigued. He could really do with some nicotine, and they would only have to stop for a couple of minutes. 'Pick me up a sausage roll as well,' he said, taking his worn, blood-stained donkey jacket off and draping it over the top half of Sam.

Sam had woken up again some moments ago, much to his disappointment as searing sparks of pain bounced back and forth through his groin. He had been desperately trying to remain still, playing dead to avoid any more beatings.

The man referred to as Mr. Benn pulled the car into the garage forecourt and got out. 'Won't be long,' he said to the man referred to as Mr. Ed. 'Don't leave this prick alone for a second. You remember what happened two-years ago?'

'Yes,' he said, rolling his eyes and huffing deeply. The man referred to as Mr. Ed hated being lectured, it was why he'd gotten into thuggery in the first place. He watched his partner amble by the pumps and into the sterile minimart as if he had all the time in the world. He wondered bitterly why it was always him left waiting in the car, watching the stiff. And they hadn't been doing as many burials as they used to. Fuck it, the man referred to as Mr. Ed thought as he decided that he needed to go for a piss. He prodded Sam in the groin to see if he was still out, then he chinned him just to be on the safe side. When he was finally satisfied that Sam was too fucked up to get up to any mischief, the man referred to as Mr. Ed slipped out of the car, and with all the stealth of a nineteen stone assassin, he made his way round the back of the minimart to the grubby, filthy forecourt toilets for that piss, and maybe even a shit if the mood took him.

Sam tried to get it together, having been presented with this sudden opportunity to save himself, which actually made him panic more. He didn't want to blow what would probably be his one chance. He began shaking his head wildly, trying to nose the man referred to as Mr. Ed's coat off his head. In a way, he was lucky that his nose was blocked and burned with vomit, otherwise he would have had to smell the man referred to as Mr. Ed's ripe odour. The coat had been soaked in the blood of a thousand beatings, and all the sweat that sort of exercise produced, not to mention all of that digging.

Sam finally slipped the coat off his head, feeling a swell of pride at having taken the first steps towards freedom. He waited for his unswollen eye to adjust to the light before being able to survey the situation and work out what to do next, until of course, he realised that he was wasting valuable seconds which he could be using to escape. His life was on the line here, he needed to think fast, he needed to multitask. He started rubbing his heels against the edge of the soft, grey backseat, trying to dislodge one of his shoes, which was no simple matter with your legs taped together.

He kicked off his left shoe without losing too much time and it thudded to the floor. Now that he had some toes free, made nimble through a lifetime of bone idleness, he clawed with them at the door handle, trying to get the bastard open. The first few attempts ended in failure and Sam began to panic again as he watched his life slipping through his hands, or feet. For once though, bucking his usual trend, Sam persevered. Sweat diluted blood poured down his face as he struggled to hook his toes onto the handle and then operate it. Finally, with a pulling and then pushing motion, he managed to get the door open, out of stupidity or pure arrogance his kidnappers hadn't bothered to put the child lock on.

Spurred on by the sense of freedom, he wriggled and squirmed his way out of the car like a lunatic. His feet fell outside the bounds of the car first, allowing him to grip and use them to pull the rest of himself out, his head smacked against the edge of the car and then rebounding onto the pavement, almost knocking him senseless again.

He began to worm his way, although his movements were more sluglike, down the street, away from the car. He knew that there was no chance he would be able to get far enough away for those two fuckers to not be able to find him. Sam's plan was to search for somewhere to hide or find someone to help. There was no one in sight though, the streets were empty, so Sam headed towards some sort of shop, or estate agents. He started forcing his head onto the dirty cold ground for leverage, hoping to speed up his journey despite the pain, occasionally picking up fag ends, chewing gum and bits of shit in his hair.

He was almost there, he was outside what did indeed turn out to be an estate agent, and through the glass of the front window he could see people moving. After the darkness, he had his first real taste of all that light he had hoped so desperately for. He began straining his neck, trying to knock his head against the window and attract someone's attention, but it vanished all too soon. A large boot hammered down onto his spine, knocking the wind out of his lungs, filling his cheeks and making his eyes near burst out as it tried to escape through his bunged-up nostrils.

'Going somewhere, cunt?' the man referred to as Mr. Benn chuckled, grinding the sole of his shoe against Sam's face.

However much pain Sam was feeling now, with this new round of blows the man referred to as Mr. Ed was administering, it couldn't compare to the damage done to his spirit. His hopes of salvation were snatched away, and he knew now that this was it, he really was going to die. As squandered as Sam's existence had been up until this point, it can't have been totally worthless because Sam wanted to live. More than anything he had ever desired in his life. He wanted to be able to see Sea-mouse again, to be yelled at by Ford, to be able to see Jane again.

He began to cry as the man referred to as Mr. Ed dragged him back to the car by his legs. He'd wet his pants, and for some reason felt embarrassed about it, like he should care if his murderers thought less of him. He wasn't struggling anymore, he just wished that this wasn't happening, he wished that he was somewhere else, that a great invisible hand would reach out, grasp him, and return him to his bed to sleep off all of this horror. They say that there are no atheists in foxholes, and for the first time in his life, Sam prayed. At his lowest point, he prayed to God that this wasn't happening, he prayed to God that He would be that invisible hand, taking him someplace else.

'We'd better get out of here quick,' the man referred to as Mr. Benn told the man referred to as Mr. Ed.

The man referred to as Mr. Benn picked Sam up with relative ease, grabbed a handful of his hair and smashed Sam's forehead into the Mondeo's wheel arch a couple of times, taking out all the frustration he felt towards his partner on the bodywork, and Sam's skull, leaving several dents. 'There's the painful way of doing this,' he said, smashing Sam's skull again, 'and then there's the even more painful way of doing this. Keep that in mind the next time you feel like taking a stroll. Either way, it's all the same to us, you're still going to end up dead.'

Sam hoped that he wasn't going to start getting philosophical on him. That was the last thing he needed, some moron's thoughts about life, polluting Sam's own last thoughts about it.

'We's only here for so much time in this world, after that, everyone ends up dead. After that, it don't matter, we's all the same, just one more set of bones. It's what yous do before yous is just one more set of bones, that's what matters. You either dish out the shit, and have fun, like me and Mr. Ed, or you are the one taking all the shit, getting all the kicks in the balls, like you. And now that we have given you this chance to know yous is going to get all the kicks to the balls, you can decide whether it's going to be a lot, by fighting us, or only a few more, by playing the game. Either ways, we's going to have our fun.' With that the man referred to as Mr. Benn dropped Sam to the ground and kicked him in the balls as a way of highlighting his point. He was just about to pick Sam up again and hurl him into the back of the car, but he didn't get the chance. The man referred to as Mr. Benn didn't see the fist coming. If he had, he would have moved out of the way. With quick, surgical precision, it caught the man referred to as Mr. Benn on the triangle of his jaw, knocking him clean out.

Sam couldn't make out what was happening or who had done this, he was still woozy from being used as a battering ram. He saw the man referred to as Mr. Ed leap forwards and heard him shout, then he saw something big throw a calm flurry of punches and heard the unmistakable sound of bone break as the man referred to as Mr. Ed's nose exploded, then there was a thud as he tumbled to the ground.

Sam felt as though someone had been listening to his prayers, divine intervention and whatnot. He felt a large, scaly, calloused hand reach out to his face and it swiftly ripped the tape from his mouth, making him glad that he had shaved this morning.

As Sam's vision started to come into focus, he slowly realised who his saviour was, destroying all his thoughts of embracing religion. No supreme, all powerful, all loving being would manifest itself in the form of a shitehawk like Riggs.

'Why the fuck did you let two pussies like that ass-fuck you like this, you cunt?' Riggs said, ripping the tape from Sam's limbs.

Why Riggs had helped him, Sam could only guess. Most likely, he had just seen it as a good reason for punching someone.

Sam forced himself up and thankfully, amazingly, he could still stand. 'Thanks,' he said, dusting himself off and then wishing he hadn't, because it hurt. Riggs didn't acknowledge him. He was busy rifling through the kidnapper's pockets, stealing their belongings, which was mostly worthless. Their watches were fakes, but they both had a fair bit of cash on them and that seemed to make Riggs happy.

'You really saved my life,' Sam said to Riggs, which although true, hadn't actually sunk in yet. To believe that you are going to die and come to accept it, and then to come out the other side took its toll on the mind. There were no moments of clarity, no newfound love of life. The world didn't suddenly appear in more vibrant and beautiful colours. It was just one big mind fuck, and your brain goes numb, and it will be hours before you realise how lucky you are and by then, the moment will have passed. You just get back to doing what you have always done, existing.

Riggs finished stealing. There was nothing in the car, which he found disappointing, but he did have two shiny new leather wallets thick with bills, so that was okay. Riggs then, ignoring Sam as being no longer of interest, went back into the minimart. He hadn't paid for his petrol when he had noticed some people to hit, and if there's one thing that Riggs wasn't, that was a thief. All the things he had taken from the kidnappers, those were spoils of war.

Sam stood there frozen for a few moments, completely dumbfounded. He stared at his assailants as they lay motionless on the floor, battered and broken. He took in their faces, the ones which would be haunting his nightmares, trying to remember every line so that there would be no confusion whenever he woke screaming in the dark.

He stood there a few moments longer. He wasn't sure where he was or what he should do. He didn't know whether he should phone the police, or maybe even kill the thugs while they were helpless. His body seemed to feel very strongly that he should get as far away from them as possible. So that was what Sam did. He clomped down the street as fast as his legs would carry him, and then he dug deep and spurred them on a bit faster, every cell in his body screaming: I want to live.

The farther he ran, Sam noticed, the less pain he felt. He wondered if finally, enough injury had been done for all those endorphins to kick in.

Chapter Seventeen

Sam finally stopped running, bent double, placed his hands on his knees to rest his weight, and then wheezed. He had been running for nearly four hours and he had been running hard. He'd been making good marathon time, at least good enough to be taken seriously as an athlete rather than one of those amateur fun runners doing it for charity. It was an even more impressive feat considering just how unfit Sam was, and how many cigarettes he had been smoking on the way, whenever he could bum one from a passerby.

It had been three hours of practically sprinting before he even knew where he was and which way he should go to get home. Then, when he did find his way back, he couldn't quite bring himself to go in. He kept expecting those thugs to leap out from behind the bushes or to smash through the door and throttle him. He wheezed at his front door for a few moments, nearly jumping out of his skin when his next-door neighbour ambled past casting him a disapproving stare. The old bastard had never liked Sam, especially since catching him one evening, vomiting rather splendidly against his new garden fence.

Sam didn't hang around long. He just kept on running not even knowing where he was heading, just wanting some place safe to crash. There must have been some subconscious reason why Sam ended up where he did.

He wheezed at Jane's front door some more before deciding to rest up on the front wall. Jane's next door neighbour ambled past, casting him a disapproving glare. The old crone had never liked Sam and disapproved of him even more after finding him one morning, vomiting rather splendidly against her new garden gnome.

Sam finally caught his breath, as well as he could, his body catching up with the stress it had been put through. He lifted his arms and had a good sniff. He stank, he really stank. A mixture of sweat and dirty, filthy fear. He wasn't at his best, that was for sure, but then that was the least of his concerns.

Sam got up from the wall and pain started to seep through his body again. When he had been running, he hadn't really noticed it, maybe because he had a purpose. As he stood up, carrying his own weight again, he felt so weak that he thought he would topple over. The muscles in his legs were burning, they seemed swollen, like they were going to burst, spraying blood, and plasma, and other juices high up into the air. His lungs felt ripped and stretched, as if someone had been using them to catch moths. He was starting to feel all those injuries again, from the multiple beatings and kicks he had been given. It was all Sam could do not to get down on his hands and knees and crawl up the path, but somehow he managed to stay on his feet, leaning against the doorway as he feebly knocked on the door.

'Oh my God, what happened to you?' Jane shrieked, as she opened the door.

'I was attacked,' he slurred, trying to get himself inside but falling instead into Jane's arms. She stepped back a couple of paces, somehow managing to hold him upright, and dragged him into the lounge, lumping him down onto the sofa. She ran into the kitchen and grabbed a clean cloth and filled a bowl with warm water. Sam tried to speak, but the words came out jumbled.

'Shh,' Jane whispered softly, starting the tough task of cleaning up Sam's face. 'You're beat up pretty bad. I think I should call an ambulance or get you to hospital or something.'

'No!' Sam yelled, finding strength from somewhere, reaching his arm out and clutching at Jane's top. 'No hospital.' Sam knew that he would be dead if he went to a hospital. They'd be looking for him there as sure as they were looking for him at his house. It wasn't safe, nowhere was, not anymore. 'People are trying to kill me,' Sam gargled. 'I've got to warn Tony and Johnny Cheung.'

Jane quietened Sam down by mopping his brow and kissing him softly on his forehead. 'You've got to get out of those dirty clothes,' Jane said, starting to unbutton his shirt. 'I'll get you into something clean and then I'll fetch you some soup.'

She stroked his hair and brushed her hand against his face, attempting to show that he was safe, and loved.

Sam winced. His cheekbone was broken or chipped and starting to balloon. Jane placed some ibuprofen in his mouth and fed him a few sips of water. It was just a gesture really and nothing more; it would take a lot more than that to dull Sam's pain and they both knew it.

'You're not filming this are you?' Sam said just as Jane was getting up to go and dig out some of his old clothes.

She turned around looking genuinely insulted. 'Jesus, is that what you think of me? I mean, look at the state of yourself, you know I'm not into any of that sick torture stuff.' She forced a smile to try and put him at ease before rushing off upstairs to root through the back of her wardrobe for some of Sam's old stuff.

When Jane came back downstairs, Sam was fast asleep. For a few seconds, she was worried that he might be dead, until she saw him twitch a little. He was clutching her phone in his hand from a failed attempt to call Tony, which Jane had to pry from his fingers.

She draped a blanket over him and tucked a cushion under his head. She washed the rest of the blood from his face and dried him off. Then, not knowing what else to do, she went into the kitchen to prepare a fresh pot of soup, popping her head into the lounge every couple of minutes to check that he was still breathing.

\#

Vince was sat at his desk. It was still early, for him at least as he normally didn't show up until late in the afternoon, but he had a lot of work to get through these next few days. Budgets to calculate, cheques to sign, locations to approve, and he still had that fourth draft of the script to read, although that was a task he would definitely be putting to one side.

When Vince had started this production company, he thought that it would be fun. A way of getting a couple of executive producer credits without having to do much. Allow him to talk in interviews about outlets for all that artistic creativity he thought he should have. It hadn't worked out like that. Vince had soon realised that this was nothing like the film industry as he knew it. He didn't just have to show up and read a few lines. This required actual effort, like running a proper business or having a proper job.

The actual output of Dirty Renegade Productions was of questionable quality to say the least. Vince's idea of edgy cinema consisting mainly of misogynistic heist movies, or misogynistic romantic comedies, all lacking in humour and originality, but with plenty of misogyny.

As a business venture, it had worked out reasonably well. All the grants available to low budget filmmakers, combined with the sheer tasteless stupidity of the movie going public, had made Vince's projects staggeringly profitable, despite the critics' hardest efforts.

Today, as he looked at the to do list his PA had made for him, Vince decided to do what he normally did when he was supposed to be getting on with the preproduction graft. He pushed the boring stuff to one side in favour of looking through the binders, thick with pictures of hopeful young actresses which agents sent him when they heard he was casting. He didn't need to do this. He had casting directors and assistants for all this sort of thing, but Vince prided himself on his attention to detail and willingness to get his hands dirty. He scrawled big asterisks with a magic marker on the women he was going to sleep with, or at least get a hand-job from, and he began touching himself slowly through his pants with his free hand. He found the whole process soothing. Just knowing that he could probably have any of the girls he wanted with the promise of a juicy part was powerfully erotic. Not that he would have to strike that bargain. He simply needed to imply it. Vince had to be careful this time though, he had already promised a major part to Leela, so sexually harassing actresses with lines could prove awkward. This particular picture, Vince was limited to slumming it with the extras.

Vince was just getting to the point where his rubbing was making his cock judder and jump about. He had to force himself to stop, having to physically pull his hand away because he really didn't want to have to change his underpants again. He decided that he would just have to finish himself off at a more convenient time. Maybe even waiting till later that evening as the constant stopping and starting, the frustrated expectation would make it feel so much better when the time finally came. He thought that maybe he would put it on Leela's forehead or possibly her chin while she was sound asleep. That always kept Vince amused for days afterwards.

'There's someone here to see you,' Gloria's voice crackled over the intercom, causing Vince to slam the portfolio books shut and zip up his trousers.

'It's Mr. David Morgan,' she buzzed through again. 'He's quite insistent. I've been trying to tell him that you're busy and unable to take visitors today, but he keeps trying to goad me into ritual suicide of some kind.'

Vince was worried, this was the last thing he was expecting from his nemesis. He'd been anticipating some sort of repercussions, now that he knew David Morgan OBE was on to him, and he'd been preparing for it. Stepping up his home security by purchasing a brand-new shovel for every room of his house to fend off any would-be attackers. But a visit from the man himself, Vince hadn't even considered. He looked around the room for possible escape routes which he knew weren't there and sighed, contemplating the lack of shovels which could only be taken as a bad omen. The office had been overlooked and Vince was mentally kicking himself for his lack of foresight. He was unprepared.

'Is anyone with him?' Vince whispered down his speaker.

'Nope, it's just him,' Gloria replied.

'No goons?' he said, still feeling uncertain. If this was some sort of hit, Vince figured that David Morgan OBE wouldn't be there when it happened, but that didn't dispel his fears. He picked up the file of girls and waved it around in front of him, jabbing with it a couple of times. The edges of the plastic binder were pretty sharp and it was quite weighty. Vince thought that he could maybe do a bit of damage with it, at least go down fighting.

'No, it's definitely just him,' Gloria's mechanised voice crackled back to him.

Vince placed the file back on his desk, inconspicuous like, within easy reach but in good jabbing range. This calmed him down a little. If David Morgan OBE tried anything funny, he would be able to get off a couple of good thrusts, maybe even cut him a little. He ruffled his hair to make sure he was looking cool and then brushed down the creases in his shirt. He leaned back in his chair and tried to look nonchalant, something he had perfected early on in his acting career, back when he was still taking shitty roles like suspect number one in cop drama number five, or back even further when it would be the likes of restaurant diner number seven.

'Okay, send the shit in,' Vince shouted, just to make sure that the shit would hear him.

David Morgan OBE strolled into Vince's office. He too was trying nonchalance but not quite pulling it off. He just looked angry and confused, which is what he was. David Morgan OBE couldn't see how it had come to this. He wanted to rip out Vince's eyes and shove them up his arse, but he couldn't. It wasn't fair. It was disgusting. It wasn't how things were supposed to work, Vince wasn't playing the game. David Morgan OBE was finding the whole business more and more distasteful the more he thought about it, and he had been thinking about it a lot. Playing out every possible scenario and permutation of actions in his mind, and each time, he came out with this as the only solution. There really was no other way, not for Vince. Vince was simply too famous. He was too valuable to too many people. Vince's time would come though, no doubt about that, when his stock wasn't riding so high, but until then, there was nothing else for it. David Morgan OBE had begrudgingly decided that he was just going to have to suck it up, go against everything that he stood for and make a deal.

'Take a seat,' Vince said, attempting to shift his character to crispy cool malevolence, trying to snatch all the power from the room and away from his adversary, the man he despised, making out that it was he, Vincent Lee who was holding all the cards, that he wasn't scared or intimidated by the man.

David Morgan OBE was still struggling with nonchalance, but his eyes gave him away. Fire burned deep behind those shiny, piggy, pinprick eyes, flames of vitriol lapping at his cornea.

David Morgan OBE slowly sat himself down on the chair opposite Vince's desk. 'At last we meet,' he said smiling menacingly, although he had hoped that it would appear friendly, a stab at building rapport.

'At last we meet,' Vince repeated, mirroring David Morgan OBE like a cheap monkey act at the zoo, staring into those burning piggy little eyes.

Their gaze didn't stray from meeting each other's eyes, neither one willing to back down and look away. It was so instinctive, so natural in both of them that neither knew why they were doing it.

'So,' Vince said, finally breaking the awkward silence, 'to what do I owe this pleasure?'

David Morgan OBE struggled, his conviction failing. He hooked his fat little fingers under his collar and loosened his tie a little. He tried to justify it to himself again. It wasn't backing down, Vince wasn't winning, it was a mutual thing. It would benefit them both equally. A simple business agreement, and you can't fuck with business no matter what your personal feelings were. There were shareholders to consider. Sometimes, you had to make sacrifices when you reached the top. 'I just thought we should meet face to face, have a little chat,' David Morgan OBE said.

Vince raised an eyebrow, it was an acting thing, two weeks of training for that little trick, but it had served him well over the years. He didn't say anything though, he didn't know what to say, he didn't know what to do with that information but raise his eyebrow, and he raised it good.

'I thought that maybe…' David Morgan OBE said, his voice wavering slightly as he had second thoughts again, third thoughts too, and maybe even fourth. 'I thought maybe we could put this silliness of the last few weeks behind us.'

Vince tried to raise his eyebrow even further, but he couldn't. He never took David Morgan OBE for the sort that would call a truce, if indeed that was what he was suggesting. 'What exactly are you offering?' Vince asked, smirking slightly. He wasn't scared anymore. Now he was feeling like he had the upper hand, like his scheme had worked and was paying dividends. He tried to suppress it though, not wanting to show all his cards, spunk his glory too soon. He tried to picture David Morgan OBE naked because for some reason he thought that would help his poker face, but it didn't. Why would it? He just sat there, grinning numbly, horrified at the images of David Morgan OBE that his mind was creating. Imagining a slow, lingering caress with David Morgan OBE, kissing him softly, pulling down his shorts and tonguing his ass. He didn't know why, he just wished that his mind would stop.

David Morgan OBE bit the bullet, and his lip. He figured that it would have to happen at some point in his life, so why not get it over and done with now. 'What I'm suggesting,' he paused, 'what I'm suggesting is that you carry on doing what you've always done, not changing a thing.'

'I'm sorry?' Vince said, not quite understanding what the hell he meant by that, still smiling like a demented freak as he tried to rid himself of those awful visions.

'You're big business Vince, you're a valuable commodity.' David Morgan OBE had to struggle with those statements, more because he knew they were true than because he had trouble flattering people he despised. 'You and me Vince, we're part of the same team. We're both entertainers, in our own way. It's the same game me and you play, and it's the only game in town. We feed the same machine and eat from the same trough.' David Morgan OBE stopped for a moment, he realised that he was in a lot of pain, his piggy little fists clenched so tight that if he didn't calm down soon, he would draw blood. 'We're just entertainers, we are only here to distract people from their shitty, humdrum little lives so they can get through the day without wrapping their belts around their necks. We're both sides of the same spectrum and together, we make colour. People don't want to wake up in the morning to hear about war, famine, and disease, or corporate takeovers. They want to open the papers, look in, and see a big dollop of sleaze, and forgive me for saying this Vince, but that's you. You're pure, unadulterated sleaze.'

Vince nodded in agreement. For a fraction of a second he had been offended, like any normal person would if they had just been called sleaze. But then he just felt proud. He imagined himself living every man's dream and wished that there were some frat-boys around he could goose and high five while secretly laughing at them as they wallowed in his testosterone, all of them hoping that one day, they too would be able to step up and follow his example.

'You're a rare breed Vince,' David Morgan OBE said, continuing his pitch. 'I don't know how or why it happens, but every once in a while, a star, a solid gold A-lister comes along who is untouchable. No matter what sleazy things you do, the public loves you. In fact, it's because of the sleazy things you do, Vince, that the public loves you. Anyone else in the public eye caught doing just a few of the things you've been doing, that would be the end of them. But not you, Vince, not you. You're the acceptable face of scandal, and do you know why? These people, your fans, and even those completely indifferent to your films, they need the odd person like you, the odd bad boy. They need to know that out there somewhere, someone is taking all the drugs, drinking all the booze, having all the unprotected sex that they don't have the stomach for. Everyone wants to live life like you, but they're too scared, so they settle for a nine to five, a new build house, maybe looking forward to half-heartedly going wild at the weekend, but they don't give it one hundred percent. The school run, walking the dog, ordering Tesco's Finest over the internet to save time, living out their rebellious fantasies vicariously through people like you. So long as you don't bore them, so long as you entertain, then we will never lose them. They will be eating out the palm of your hand, and I'll be the one throwing you the nuts.'

Vince was still nodding in agreement, like one of David Morgan OBE's goons. He hadn't heard anything he could disagree with yet. It all seemed fairly reasonable. But he was still wondering what the cunt, the dirty fucking bastard, the man he hated, wanted. 'So what exactly are you suggesting?' Vince said, raising his intonation towards the end to indicate that it was a question, as if the phrasing and question mark wasn't enough.

'What I am suggesting,' David Morgan OBE chuckled falsely, like the sort of creep he usually fired, handing a copy of the samurai code out as the poor sap left. 'A solution, that's what I'm suggesting. Something which will make us both happy and keep the cash rolling in. All I want you to do, is keep on doing everything and everyone you've always done, and I'll keep on doing what I've always done, printing what you've done on the front page. All that I ask is that you stop all of these stupid investigations.'

Vince laughed out loud, half acting, half spontaneously. David Morgan OBE wasn't bothered though, he had expected that reaction, it was all part of the game, the only game in town. You couldn't just come out with what you wanted, David Morgan OBE knew that much. You had to take them on a journey, you had to make out like the other person was in charge, like it was them doing you the favour by agreeing to your terms.

'Why would I want to stop my investigations?' Vince asked, sounding about as cocky as a person could sound, which was very cocky indeed. The eyebrow still firmly raised, hovering and ready for action.

'Well, for one thing,' David Morgan OBE said coolly, 'I've already broken your team up. We've had a minor setback with one of them, but the other two should be dealt with shortly, and then it's just a case of mopping up the straggler,' David Morgan OBE said, smiling menacingly. He was on safe ground with that sort of expression, smiling menacingly, it was all part of the job, a tool of his trade, something he used like a pen or laptop.

Vince didn't respond in any noticeable way. He was still trying to play it cool. He knew what David Morgan OBE meant by that, of course he did, it was obvious.

'And secondly,' David Morgan OBE continued, 'we can make this work for both of us. I'm talking about pulling together, pitching in for the common good. We might not like each other, we've both done some bad things, although what you did to my mother was infinitely worse than anything I have said about you.' David Morgan OBE was clenching his chubby little fists once more.

Vince had to stop himself from laughing again. He didn't feel guilty about that one little bit. He felt proud, and it was highly satisfying to see firsthand how cut up David Morgan OBE was about it.

'We can make things better for both of us if we just work together,' David Morgan OBE said. 'As much as you might not like it, I'm not going to stop printing stories about you in my newspaper. No one in my position would. It makes good copy, and it's in my readers best interests, because it interests them.'

'That doesn't seem like much of a deal,' Vince said, as sharp as ever.

'Well, that's where you are wrong,' David Morgan OBE chuckled. 'Like I said, this will be good for us both. It seems to me that the stuff that we make up is not what bothers you, it certainly doesn't seem to bother anyone else. In my experience, most celebrities take it as a compliment that we're so desperate to keep their name in print that we're willing to make shit up about them. What I'm suggesting is that when we have a story, a proper story, we'll come to you first, only publish at the right time. You have a new film coming out, great, then we'll go to press with some juicy scandals. No matter what the story is, you know deep down that it can only be good for you, and me of course. And if anything is too bad, if it's going to cause you too many problems, we won't run it. Like I said, we'll be working together. Think of the potential. You can use us just as much as we use you, fifty-fifty. And of course, no matter what the story is, it will be written so you still come off looking cool.

Men will still want to be you and women will still want to be with you, as the saying goes.'

Vince took it all in, both men staring at each other without speaking for another uncomfortably long period of time. Vince was mulling the idea over in his head. The basic concept seemed sound in principle. They would play the game together, the only game in town, on the same team. It could work out beautifully, most profitable indeed, so long as David Morgan OBE stuck to the rules and actually did come to him first with all the stories before he ran them. He started to see all the possibilities of an agreement like this.

'So, for example,' Vince pondered aloud, 'if I was cheating on a girlfriend and you had proof, you would only print it when I was bored of her and wanted to dump the bitch?' Vince wasn't bored of Leela yet, but something like this could certainly make his life easier in the future.

'That's right,' David Morgan OBE said. 'We'll print stuff about you cheating anyway, but we'll make sure that the dates don't add up, so that you always have an alibi. Then, if you want to get rid of her, then we just print real story after real story, until she can't take anymore. And not just that, I can guarantee that your films will all get rave reviews, and more publicity than they would normally. We'll cobble together some bullshit stories, you know the drill. And if someone pisses you off, well we can slam them, it'll be fun.

We'll keep the public in sleaze and maybe, just maybe, we can put all this nonsense behind us.'

Vince laughed a little again, but this time he wasn't trying to mock David Morgan OBE, he was just thinking how well this would work out. He realised now that he would be untouchable. He could do anything he wanted and get away with it. He could pretty much do that before, but now, now he would have one of the largest press organisations behind him. It was a licence to have fun. No more looking over his shoulder. There was still that nagging little voice at the back of his head telling him that David Morgan OBE couldn't be trusted.

'And all I need to do in return is stop my investigations?' Vince asked.

'They don't benefit anyone, they certainly haven't affected my sales much. If anything, these adverts you've been running have actually helped us. I guess people are so used to negative advertising now, that they just assumed it was some pretentious stunt we were pulling.'

Vince nodded noncommittally. 'Go on,' he said.

'And I also ask that you forget all about those chumps you hired, forget you ever saw them, forget they ever existed. I can assure you that they will be dealt with by the end of the day.'

Again, Vince nodded, although this time less noncommittally and more like he was agreeing. He realised now that he had never wanted to keep his name out of the papers, he just wanted to control it. It was a little disappointing that he wasn't going to see his revenge to completion. But this was an opportunity too good to let slide. If Hollywood had taught him anything, it was when to make and break allegiances. Fuck people over with smiles. David Morgan OBE would get his, sooner or later.

Vince put on a big wide smile, but it was more than that. Dimples in the right place, lines perfectly symmetrical, flashing those perfect pearly whites, worth about sixty grand in cosmetic dental surgery and countless millions in poster campaigns. It was a matinee idol's smile. The dreams of a couple of million souls locked up in the contortions of a few dozen tiny muscles. 'You got yourself a deal,' Vince said theatrically, breathing right so that his words bounced off every corner of the room and crevice of David Morgan OBE's body. He held out his hand and David Morgan OBE leant forward to shake on it with his sweaty little chubby mitts. They shook, and then Vince wiped his hand on his trousers. Vince was just the cheesy sort of fucker to think or say something along the lines of: if you can't beat them, join them, or maybe: keep your friends close, but your enemies closer, but quite frankly, he lacked the imagination. David Morgan OBE on the other hand, didn't.

'If you can't beat them, join them!' David Morgan OBE said, standing to get up. 'We'll do lunch sometime, finalise the deal,'

'Wait, where are you going?' Vince said, still smiling. 'This calls for a celebration.' He pulled open a desk drawer and produced a small, square mirror with a couple of grams of high-quality cocaine piled up in a sort of pyramid. Of all of Vince's vices, drugs were not the greatest one, but when it came to moments like this, moments of real power brokerage, it seemed like the thing to do. A show of affluence, conspicuous consumerism; there was nothing like doing a couple of lines of coke to say, this is how rich I am and this is how much money we can piss away together.

David Morgan OBE sat down again. He didn't really want to, but when it came to closing a deal, he was prepared to go above and beyond.

Vince lay the mirror on his desk, opened up a brand-new pack of standard issue playing cards and pulled out the Ace of Spades, which he then used to cut a small section from the pile of class A. No credit cards for Vince when he was preparing drugs, he always thought that credit cards just lacked class, even if it was gold or platinum. A clean, crisp Ace of Spades was just so much cooler. He started to cut the smaller pile into neat little lines, uniform in length and width. He pulled out a hundred-dollar bill from his wallet, which was only in his wallet for this very purpose, and he carefully rolled it up into a tight tube and took a hit in each nostril.

Vince handed the cylindrical bill to David Morgan OBE who clumsily manipulated it with his chubby little pinkies. He eyeballed the powder encrusted layer of Vince's snot glistening under the unnatural light and shuddered. He tightened the tube and stuffed it up his nose, placing it at the end of one of the lines and awkwardly sniffing it up, as if someone were offering him a jar of something weird and out of date to smell. The drug hit him almost instantly. It didn't make him feel on top of the world, like he'd just sent hundreds of men off to their deaths, and it didn't suddenly make him feel like he was number one, like he was the only worthwhile person in the world, because he already felt like that anyway. It just made him feel a bit fuzzy, like he had to sneeze, or ejaculate, or both.

'We have a deal then?' David Morgan OBE sneezed, his eyes watering and turning pink as he also ejaculated. 'You're going to forget about these nobodies, as if you never met them?'

Vince nodded and then took another line of the overpriced white shit. 'Yeah baby,' he said, 'we're going to do fine together.'

Chapter Eighteen

Tony fumbled around with the key in the lock while Johnny Cheung kicked idly at the wall. He pushed open the office door and shooed the day's mail out of the way.

Johnny Cheung put the kettle on for a brew, something he'd been craving for the last few hours stuck in the Mercedes with nothing but his business partner's farts to warm him.

Tony sat down at his desk and kicked off his shoes, stretching his large frame and yawning loudly. 'You know,' he said thoughtfully, 'he struck me as the sort of person who would have at least told us if he had decided to quit. I know he was having a cunt of a time on that stakeout, and some of the other cunting things we've been doing for that cunt, but even so, I don't think he would have just walked out on us.'

'I hope he isn't dead,' Johnny Cheung said, sipping at his steaming cup of tea which he was holding with both hands. 'I was really starting to like that guy.'

'Me too. That cunt was all right.'

Johnny Cheung sat down at his desk and started to type up the day's report, not that there was much to report. David Morgan OBE came to work, left for a bit, came back, left again, and didn't come back. It was more of a receipt for Vince than anything, a little bit of proof that they were really there, outside David Morgan OBE's office all day.

'You think maybe we should try phoning him again?' Johnny Cheung said, looking up from his computer screen.

'I already have,' Tony said. He did feel genuinely concerned for Sam, praying that he hadn't gotten the poor bastard killed over something as worthless as this. Tony, in his life, professional and otherwise, had gotten several people killed. At least, that was the way he had always seen it, ripping himself up inside with guilt. He hadn't really gotten anyone killed, he had just been there when bad things had happened, unable to help. But natural leader that he was, Tony always stepped up and took personal responsibility in his mind. 'It was just that cunting answer phone again.'

Johnny Cheung finished his tea. He was about to make another when the sound of breaking glass and splintering wood made him and Tony jump. They looked over to see someone battering the remains of the unlocked door to pieces, rather unnecessarily.

The man referred to as Mr. Ed's face was smashed and swollen. He was sporting two black eyes and a dirty, self-applied plaster cast to try and repair what was left of his nose. He smiled grimly at Tony and Johnny Cheung, showing off his newly missing front teeth. The man referred to as Mr. Benn quickly slipped in behind the man referred to as Mr. Ed, his jaw hanging down, misshapen and deformed, making him look mildly undead. In unison, the two men pulled out large, oily hunting knives, the sort designed for gutting deer after a fresh kill. Sturdy, practical fuckers that could be used again and again without the danger of breaking.

Tony, who was always fast to read a situation, leapt up, throwing his chair overhead at the man referred to as Mr. Ed, knocking him backwards. He looked over at Johnny Cheung as if to say: 'Here we go again,' and then jumped up onto his desk, bellowing a war cry consisting mainly of the word cunt. The man referred to as Mr. Benn slashed at him, leaping forward with all his weight. But Tony was too fast, managing to jump over him, swing round, and knee him up the arse.

The man referred to as Mr. Benn buckled over onto Tony's desk, mewling in pain. The man referred to as Mr. Ed, who had now gotten himself back up and dusted off the bigger bits of chair, grabbed Tony from behind, trying to get him into a half nelson as Tony tried to shake him off. Johnny Cheung lunged at them like a crazy person, brandishing a lamp in one hand and his Gameboy in the other. He smashed the lamp into the man referred to as Mr. Ed's temple. He followed it up with a fierce crack to the eyeball with his Gameboy and brought the stem of the lamp down onto the man referred to as Mr. Ed's big fat head. The man referred to as Mr. Ed stumbled enough to let go of Tony. Johnny Cheung took advantage, leaping onto the man referred to as Mr. Ed's back, attempting to strangle the cunt. Tony ducked out of the way and threw the man referred to as Mr. Ed to the floor, Johnny Cheung included.

The man referred to as Mr. Benn had gotten up off the desk, tears still dribbling from his eyes. He swept his knife up from the floor and lunged at Tony, but Tony saw it coming which was why he moved out of the way. Just at the last moment, he slipped round the side of the man referred to as Mr. Benn, meeting him with a quick, powerful side palm strike to the neck, collapsing the man referred to as Mr. Benn's trachea. The man referred to as Mr. Benn fell backwards, almost in slow motion, clutching at his throat, gasping and gagging for breath. He was kicking his legs about and writhing all over the floor, his mouth flapping open and shut like a cheap, inbred fairground goldfish. Tony looked at him, looked at his face, at what he'd done with little or no emotion but the briefest grin of satisfaction. The man referred to as Mr. Benn showed a lot of emotion. Pure fear, and hate. In a few minutes, he would be dead, and there was nothing he could do, or anything anyone around him would do about it. So he just flapped and flopped about as he died of strangulation, feeling somehow like he was drowning, like he was underwater, completely helpless to save himself, but he wasn't underwater, he wasn't drowning, he was slowly choking to death on a dirty, seldom cleaned office floor.

The man referred to as Mr. Ed had shaken Johnny Cheung off and kicked him across the room. He charged at Tony, knocking him backwards with a shoulder barge. 'I'm going to tear yous twos fucking faces off,' he said, gripping his hunting knife tightly and taking a step forward. Tony didn't react other than to brace himself, raising his thick arms for defence. The man referred to as Mr. Ed slashed at him twice, left to right, trying to disembowel him, but Tony jumped back with surprising agility. The man referred to as Mr. Ed didn't let up for an instant. He attacked again, this time stabbing the knife down at Tony's chest, but Tony grabbed his wrist just in time, just as the blade was about to pierce his flesh. The man referred to as Mr. Ed went to punch him with his other arm, but Tony grabbed that too. They struggled like that, a force of strength, an old school grapple, the strings of their necks straining through their skin as each hulk of a man tried to gain the upper hand. Tony summoned up all the strength he had been saving in reserve and pushed and pulled the man referred to as Mr. Ed about, knocking him onto the desk before they both tumbled to the ground, the man referred to as Mr. Ed somehow managing to land on top. Drips of sweat and blood from the man referred to as Mr. Ed landed in Tony's mouth as he tried desperately to stick the knife in Tony's chest, and while Tony tried desperately to stop him. The blade of the knife seemed to remain static an inch above Tony's chest as it was forced up and then back down again a millimetre at a time.

'I'm going to kill you,' the man referred to as Mr. Ed said, either trying to spur himself on or simply make sure that there was no misunderstanding as to what he was trying to achieve. Tony didn't waste his energy on talking or cursing back, he barely even noticed that the man referred to as Mr. Ed had said anything at all. Tony's energy was taken up trying to stop the cunt from killing him, and then maybe, hopefully, it could be used to snap his neck.

Johnny Cheung shot up, he had only been on the floor for a couple of seconds. He saw what was happening, Tony was in serious trouble, and he let out an ear-piercing cry with words incomprehensible to anyone. He charged towards Tony and the man referred to as Mr. Ed, aiming to save the greatest friend he had ever had from being stabbed through the heart. He was going to dive for the man referred to as Mr. Ed, kick the knife out of his hands and then kick him to death.

It was with a sprint like burst of explosive force that Johnny Cheung charged, his expression so fearsome that warriors of old would have been proud, and afraid. He was building up speed when something tripped him up. The man referred to as Mr. Benn, who had now turned blue, in a last desperate action, the last thing he would ever do in this world, which much like the way he lived the rest of his life involved hurting somebody, had reached out and grabbed Johnny Cheung's ankle causing him to hit the ground. He hit the ground so hard that instantly he was knocked clean out. Whether the man referred to as Mr. Benn did this out of a sense of duty to his partner, or out of revenge, or simply to fulfil his own sick need to inflict pain, no one will ever know, but it didn't really matter, the result was still the same.

Ever loyal, in his unconscious state Johnny Cheung was still trying to fight, to protect Tony, laying down his own life if need be. In his unconscious hallucinations, like a one man killing machine, a living incarnation of the god of war, he'd stomped the remaining life out of the man referred to as Mr. Benn's face, wiped his shoe on the carpet before running over to the man referred to as Mr. Ed, ripping the knife out of his hands and using it to slash him to bits, hooking him on the floor with a couple of dirty tricks he learnt as a cop, popping his shoulder out of its socket and then popping it back in again, making his last moments as painful as possible. But he didn't do any of that, he was unconscious. He just lay there, a few globs of dribble pooling at the side of his mouth.

\#

When Johnny Cheung came to, a few minutes later, things had certainly turned into one hell of a pickle. Johnny Cheung found himself soaked in something sticky and warm. His first thought after regaining consciousness was Tony. He shot up and began his charge where he had left off, as if he had been momentarily put on pause, but as he tried to run, he found that he wasn't getting anywhere. his feet just slipped and skidded about as his legs swung back and forth, finally tumbling slowly back to the ground. As he fell, his eyes darted forward to Tony and what they saw made his heart skip a beat and made him wish that it skipped a few more, possibly never making a tune ever again. Tony was lying perfectly still, his skin as pale as death. The man referred to as Mr. Ed was lying almost on top of him, as if they were engaged in some sort of post-coital embrace. As Johnny Cheung landed with a splash, he realised what it was he had slipped in and his stomach turned to lead and his heart skipped a couple more beats. The whole floor was literally flooded with blood, an unholy sea of red. It looked like there was gallons of the stuff giving the office the look of an unlicensed, unhygienic abattoir floor. Johnny Cheung crawled through the gore as fast as he could. When he finally got to his friend he couldn't bare it. He was heartbroken. He tried to roll the man referred to as Mr. Ed off but he couldn't. Even though his neck had been snapped in one clean and unfortunately practiced motion, the big old bastards' cold dead hand still gripped stubbornly to the handle of his hunting knife, which was embedded deep in Tony's guts. That wasn't the biggest concern for Johnny Cheung though, the knife was blocking the flow of blood from that particular wound. What concerned Johnny Cheung was the fucking huge open wound next to the stuck knife. The open wound was the one blood was pissing from, although now it was becoming more of a trickle. The change in Tony made Johnny Cheung weep, the tears streaming down his face. Tony was still alive,

Johnny Cheung was thankful for that, but he had seen enough victims to know that it wouldn't be for long. He had lost too much blood. Tony looked old, and weak. His life force, his energy, his youthful vitality had drained away along with the majority of his bodily fluids. Tony moved his eyes, he didn't have the energy to move anything else. The strongest man Johnny Cheung had ever known too feeble to move a muscle bigger than a pea. His eyes stared into Johnny Cheung and he gave off the faintest hint of a smile, although it could well have been some sort of reflex reaction to the five-inch blade tapping gently at his spinal column.

Tony shivered. He was cold, deathly cold from all that piping hot blood he had lost. Johnny Cheung crawled around to the other side of him, away from the ugly cadaver stuck to his partner. He cradled Tony's head in his lap, being careful to be as gentle as possible. Tony looked so frail and fragile that Johnny Cheung was scared he might shatter. His face seemed thin to Johnny Cheung, as if he had lost a lot of weight in just a few minutes, which he had.

Tony moved his eyes again slowly, something that used to be so simple was now obviously, something of a struggle, as if now his eyeballs were no longer lumps of goo, but something much heavier. He took a while, but finally he managed to focus on Johnny Cheung once more and seemed to muster a look of recognition. He gave a weak smile to his old friend. A dark red trickle of blood emerged from the corner of his pale mouth contrasting horrifically against his pasty skin. 'I'm so cold,' Tony whispered, so meekly it sent Johnny Cheung over the edge and he could no longer hold back another flood of tears from pouring down his face.

'Shhh… shhh…' Johnny Cheung said with a soothing tone of voice, stroking Tony's hair lovingly, trying to comfort him as best he could in his dying moments. 'Everything is going to be okay.'

Tony coughed. 'Tell David Morgan…' he wheezed, staring deep into Johnny Cheung's watery eyes,' 'tell David Morgan that he's a cunt!'

Tony coughed again and a lump of snot-like clotted blood landed on Johnny Cheung's chin, but he didn't move to wipe it away.

'Everything is going to be ok,' Johnny Cheung said again; he couldn't think of anything else to say. He took his jacket off and draped it over Tony, but it was nothing more than a gesture. The size discrepancy made trying to cover Tony with Johnny Cheung's jacket just ridiculous, like trying to hide a stud horses' shame with a postage stamp. But mainly, it was nothing more than a gesture because Tony would never be warm again. It made Johnny Cheung feel better because it was actively doing something and in turn, that made Tony feel better, not that he could feel much of anything anymore, except for the cold.

Tony's eyes started to roll back in their sockets as the last remaining drops of blood in his brain drained away and everything began to shut down, never to be started back up again. You could almost see his life being sucked out of his body. He convulsed with surprising force for a few moments and rather than a death rattle, he just sucked in one last breath with a strange squeaking noise. 'I'm glad you were my friend,' Tony managed to gasp. Then he was still.

Chapter Nineteen

It was around one o'clock in the afternoon when Sam finally woke up. For about five minutes he felt refreshed, like he'd had a good night's sleep and was ready for anything. He thought about getting some toast and a cup of tea, maybe even some high fibre breakfast cereal. Then the pain hit him again and that felt bad. He could almost cope with it though, it was just pain, you could tune it out or at least get used to it. But then the panic returned, small waves of dread at first, building up into one massive tsunami of despair as yesterday's memories began to return like unwanted pets. This was worse than any hangover Sam had ever experienced, and he hadn't even been drinking, although he wished that he had. It took him a few moments to realise that he wasn't in his own bed, and a few moments more to realise that he was actually lying on a sofa, quilted in a lovely, comfy, snuggly warm quilt. It took a further few moments for his seriously compromised brain to make the connection of where he had ended up the day before, that he was lying on Jane's sofa, quilted in her lovely, comfy, snuggly warm quilt. He started to calm down and relax as he kicked his bare feet against the comforting fabric, happily finding a cosy pocket of warmth.

He realised that he was wearing clean clothes, mostly his old ones discarded at Jane's house and never collected, but they felt fresh against his skin and he could still smell that friendly smell of fabric conditioner. The soiled ones from the day before were piled neatly on the floor beside the sofa. They had been cleaned and pressed and they too had a comforting, friendly smell of fabric conditioner emanating from them. He rubbed his throbbing head and found that his cuts and scrapes had been covered with several plasters and a bandage was wrapped tightly around his forehead.

Jane was slouched in a chair opposite him. She was half asleep, her eyes flickering open and closed. She yawned before getting up and walking over to Sam, forcing him to lie back down and wrapping him up snugly in the quilt again. 'You need to rest,' she said, sitting down almost on top of him. 'You're going to have to spend a lot of time laid up until you're fully recovered.' She stroked his hair before leaning over to kiss him on the forehead. Sam curled up into the foetal position., all warm and cosy. He felt safe for the first time in a long while. Nothing bad could happen to him while he was being cared for like this.

'Are you hungry?' she asked, sounding just as concerned and matronly as before, stroking his hair with one hand and sneakily running her other hand under the covers and up Sam's inner thigh. Sam was half asleep and his body was too numb to notice what she was doing, until her hand, cold against his swollen and burning skin, reached his sorry looking testicles. For about a second he considered it, then he shivered with pain as he woke up again fully.

'What are you doing?' he groaned, helplessly trying to fend her off. Each time he managed to slap her away she'd gently replace her hand, as persistent as ever.

'C'mon,' she said cheerfully, hoping the positive attitude might aid his recovery, 'it will make you feel better.' She slyly slipped a thumb up his anus and Sam was too weak to stop her.

Sam whimpered as he felt tight, rhythmic pressure against his prostrate. 'I can't even think about sex at a time like this. I can't think about anything.'

She sensed the despair in his voice as he lay there looking like he was about to burst into tears. She had never seen him broken like this. He was broken last night of course, but that was just injuries, there was still fight in him. Now on the other hand, it was like he had given up. Like he was just willing to lay down and take it until he stopped breathing.

Jane jammed her thumb further up his arse to get more leverage, trying to shock some life back into him. She bent down, ducking under the covers to nuzzle his crotch with her face. She was trying, with the best of intentions, to help as she slipped his swollen – but not swollen in a good way - penis into her mouth.

Sam was torn, and the pain was such that he thought his ball sack might be too. What Jane was doing was starting to feel pretty good, but then he was still in so much agony that it was gumming up his senses so that any pleasure he was experiencing was having to take a back seat. There were other concerns starting to return to him also. 'Stop it!' he cried, regaining some strength, trying to pull Jane from his genitals.

'What's the matter?' Jane asked looking up and licking her lips. 'You can put it anywhere.'

Normally Sam would leap at the chance, but now wasn't the time, there was too much at stake. He had to get in touch with Tony and Johnny Cheung, that was priority number one.

'Stop!' Sam cried again, tugging lightly at a handful of Jane's hair. Sam reached around Jane and managed to grab the phone off the coffee table by the side of the sofa, Jane's mouth still firmly clamped to his genitalia. 'Now really isn't the time,' Sam whimpered as he tried to dial the office while still attempting to tug Jane off, and Jane still attempting to tug him off. He finally managed to get the correct combination of numbers punched into the phone, but no luck. It just rang five times and then went straight to the answer phone and Tony's unforgettable cunting message.

Jane was licking the tip again, something that would normally be making Sam go cross-eyed. He tried Tony's mobile but no joy, it was switched off, Johnny Cheung's too. He started a whole new batch of panicking, fearing the worst for his colleagues, which although Sam didn't know it, was fully justified. He quickly tried all three lines again with the same results and his stomach once more rumbled with shit stirring fear. He had to get in touch with Tony and Johnny Cheung. They would be able to lead, tell him what to do, where to go, how to be safe. A lifetime of apathy had made Sam lost when it came to serious situations. True, he was lost in most situations, unless it involved ordering a drink, but a situation that had life changing consequences, especially when those life changing consequences could mean changing from being living to being dead, Sam just didn't have the experience to cope. He needed someone to tell him what to do.

\#

There was a knock at the door and then the doorbell rang.

'Don't get it,' Sam cried, what watery shit he had starting to back up to his ring-piece.

Jane looked up, wiping cock juice from her mouth with her forearm. 'Don't be stupid,' Jane said, 'no one knows you're here. And don't you think that if someone was here to kill you, they wouldn't bother knocking?'

Sam looked around for a weapon, clutching a shoe to his chest pathetically, like it was Excalibur itself.

Jane got up and straightened her clothing before heading off to get the door.

'Don't get it,' Sam hissed again, grabbing at her arm, tugging her back to him. He was starting to drip in sweat as that stodgy feeling of imminent death and hopelessness returned, images of yesterday's beatings flashing through his mind like a violent, underground flick book.

'Relax,' she said, pressing a finger to his lips. 'I'm expecting a package today, it's probably that.'

Sam couldn't take it. He didn't want to know what was waiting for him behind that door. He had a bad feeling about this. The whole place was starting to stink of death, not that Sam could smell much with his busted nasal passage, and he really didn't want it busted up anymore. He managed to roll himself off the sofa and curled up behind it, shoe in hand.

Jane peeked to see if Sam was all right and then opened the front door, expecting to see some bored looking bastard with a parcel for her, but it wasn't. Jane had never seen him before, and she didn't like the look of him, with his piggy little eyes. He certainly wasn't here with a delivery, not in that expensive suit. Sam recognised him though, he knew who it was right away, and cowered as he peeked round the side of the sofa, with his shoe.

Jane was just about to ask who the hell it was and what the hell he wanted, but the impatient bastard didn't give her the chance, barging past her like he owned the place, not that he felt he would want to. He screwed his face in disgust as he looked around Jane's house. Flat pack furniture that passes for designer with the common masses, cheap prints hung on the walls as if they were quality pieces of art. To David Morgan

OBE, it seemed tacky. He was eyeballing more and more items with ever increasing amounts of repulsion looking like these people's bad taste had left a bad taste in his mouth. He had never thought that people really lived like this, it was as if someone were playing some sort of a joke on him.

'Who do you think you are, storming in here like that?' Jane asked. She was trying to act calm and composed. He didn't look like a thug. His hands hadn't seen the sort of manual labour involved in beating a human to death. they were too well moisturised, and small.

'Where is he?' David Morgan OBE barked.

'Who?' Jane answered innocently, with an almost heroic attempt at playing dumb.

'Listen bitch,' David Morgan OBE snapped, knocking some ornaments over with a quick backhand to show that he was serious. 'I'm not here to fuck around, where is he?'

'I don't know who you are or what you want, but I think you've got the wrong place,' Jane stuttered, knowing full well that he hadn't got the wrong place and wondering what it was exactly that Sam had managed to get her into.

'I know that he's fucking here,' David Morgan OBE shouted up at the ceiling, in case he was upstairs.

Jane was about to come back with some witty remark or facetious comment to try and tempt him out of her house, but it was no longer necessary, Sam had begun to crawl out from behind the sofa on his hands and painfully, on his knees.

'I think it's me you're looking for,' Sam said slowly, still crawling like a dog. He stood himself up, trying to regain a bit of composure, like dusting himself off a bit would stop him from looking completely ridiculous after that little display.

'You don't know how long it has taken me to find you,' David Morgan OBE said with a forced chuckle, trying to seem friendly, to mask how angry he was at Sam. Of course he was annoyed that it had come to this, but he was slightly amused too. He had that warm, powerful feeling coursing through his veins which always came to David Morgan OBE when he was about to change someone's life, making all their dreams come true, giving something that they had always wanted that only he had the power to grant, which would, in turn, give rise to the even more powerful feeling of being able to yank it all away from them any time he felt like it. 'Eight hours. That's how long it has taken me to find you,' he stated, for some reason Sam failed to understand. 'Which as you know, in the newspaper business, is a long time.'

Sam was kind of confused. He was trying to work out what the hell the man was banging on about. He kept looking around the room and then glancing back at the front door, expecting those two murderers to barge their way in, or maybe some other sort of masked assailants to leap out from somewhere, ready to pop a bullet through his medulla oblongata after inflicting a smorgasbord of blows to his testicles.

'Do you mind telling me who the fuck you are?' Jane demanded, storming over to position herself between Sam and David Morgan OBE.

David Morgan OBE grinned at her darkly, before grinning at Sam in an even more sinister fashion, as if to say, 'do you want to tell her?'

'That's him,' Sam whimpered, 'That's David Morgan.'

Jane looked him up and down. She'd heard a lot about David Morgan OBE, especially recently, but she wasn't sure what she had been expecting. Someone meaner looking, uglier maybe. He did seem like a bastard though. She looked back at Sam, looked him up and down and wondered if it was the podgy fucker in her house with silly little hands and piggy eyes that could have been responsible. Seeing Sam in such a state with the probable culprit so close by stirred something violent within her. She leaped forward at David Morgan OBE, landing one almighty slap across his exfoliated cheeks, digging her nails in as much as possible.

David Morgan OBE rubbed his silly little hand against his cheek, dumb founded by not only the shock of it, that someone would have the audacity to strike him, but also by the stinging pain of the blow. He reacted in the way he thought most appropriate for a man of his position and status. He smiled wickedly at Jane before punching her full in the face, knocking her backwards. He felt the sting on his cheek again and just couldn't stop himself from striking her again, following up the first blow while she was still reeling with a vicious backhand.

Watching in horror as David Morgan OBE knocked the wind out of her, Sam was reminded of a joke Sexfiend had once told him about beating women, before bursting out in hysterics and slapping his secretary jovially about the face and then again on the bottom. Sam didn't know why he had just thought of that, it was wholly inappropriate. Jane was being assaulted by a man who was probably here to kill them both.

Sam tried to help but his legs gave way and he fell back to the floor in front of David Morgan OBE. 'How did you find me?' Sam snivelled uncontrollably. No one but his closest friends knew about Jane.

David Morgan OBE pushed Jane to the floor as she squatted, gasping for breath. He chuckled to himself before turning slowly, darkly towards Sam and laughing again. He stopped laughing for a few moments, allowing time for the full force of his laugh to sink in before laughing at him again, forcefully. 'How did I find you?' he chuckled. 'I'm the editor of Britain's top selling newspaper, finding people is what we fucking do.'

Sam looked over at Jane writhing about on the floor and wished that he hadn't gotten her mixed up in all of this. 'What is it you want from me?' Sam asked, the dread hanging in his voice like plague germs.

David Morgan OBE laughed out loud again, with his smug expression and his forced laugh to make sure that Sam knew that it was he, David Morgan OBE, who had all of the power in this room. 'To quote your former employer,' he said smugly, 'I could have you killed. You do know that don't you?'

Sam did know that, of course he knew that it was a stupid question, he just had to look at himself in the mirror to know that David Morgan OBE could have him killed.

'But I don't want to have you killed, not anymore,' David Morgan OBE said, his smug grin looking smugger than ever.

Sam looked up, a pathetic grain of hope in his eyes, quickly disappearing as he wondered what the worse thing that David Morgan OBE was going do was.

'Despite what you have done to me,' David Morgan OBE continued, 'despite the shitty rotten things that you personally have done to me, I am willing to be lenient.'

A few more grains of hope returned, fighting a losing battle with the expectation of death.

'I can tell by your gormless expression that you don't believe me,' David Morgan OBE told Sam, somehow managing to squeeze out a little more smugness.

Sam shook his head in defeat, thinking that this was it, this was where he gets told the ins and outs of his own death.

'No, I'm not going to have you killed,' David Morgan OBE said, starting to pace up and down the room, strutting like he owned the world, and the moon. 'I'm not going to have you killed because I have decided to offer you a job.' He paused for a moment to allow that revelation to sink in, but it didn't sink in. Sam couldn't begin to comprehend this man offering him a job, the man who had already told him to fuck off in one interview only a few weeks ago. The man whose mother Sam had only recently made weep like a child, cursing his name to the bottom reaches of hell. His jaw dropped, maybe from the shock, maybe because it was partially dislocated.

David Morgan OBE seemed to read his mind, or perhaps he was just continuing with his proposal regardless. 'I'm not going to kill you and I am offering you a job. A good job too, investigative reporter no less. The full package: pension, company car, a fucking generous six figure annual salary. A dream come true.' He paused again for sinking in time, but he shouldn't have for it gave Sam a few moments to really think about it. Sam would have been a fool to say that it wasn't tempting, he wasn't quite sure how much was meant by six figures but it sounded like a lot of money. But that didn't matter, not really. He didn't care about the money. He thought about what it would mean and it was no dream come true, working for that cunt David Morgan OBE. Then there was everything he had been doing these last few weeks, following journos around. He just couldn't imagine himself becoming one of them again, especially David Morgan OBE's sort of journalist. The hypocrisy of it all, commenting on others when they were no better than junkies and thieves themselves. People with problems and vices, weaknesses just like every other son-of-a bitch on the planet. It was a joke, one great big insane joke. And then of course there was going to be some sort of a catch. There was always a catch. Like he was just being lulled into a false sense of security and when he felt safe, like everything was going fine, out comes the hacksaw and pliers.

'I'm offering you a job young man,' David Morgan OBE said, puffing himself up like he was performing some sort of birdlike display, attempting to land a mate. 'I'm not offering you this because I like you. In fact, I hate you. No, I'm offering you this opportunity because if I'd have known what you were capable of, I would have hired you on the spot. You've got what it takes. You could go far. I know it's hard to believe, but I started my life as an investigative reporter, it was my first job. Someone who has done the things that you have done to me has definitely got what it takes, you've already proved yourself. I haven't been this impressed by a young journalist for a long time. I'm earmarking you for great things. Play your cards right and things could be very good for you.'

Sam was a little less shocked now. It would take someone who was as big an asshole as David Morgan OBE to respect what Vince had had him doing. 'I already have a job,' Sam said defiantly, 'I don't need another.'

Now it was David Morgan OBE's turn to be shocked. He wasn't expecting that response, that was not the normal response when he offered someone a job. He didn't buy it. He just figured that the little bastard was even more sly than he had given him credit for. He figured he was angling for more money, it was the only thing that made any sense. No one turned down David Morgan OBE. No one. 'Ok, fair enough, I've got a good feeling about you. I'm willing to go another ten grand. Plus, bonuses. This is a once in a lifetime offer. You're not going to make this sort of money anywhere else, and like I said, I think you could go far. We need people who aren't going to start crying at the first whiff of phone tapping or something else distasteful.' He raised an eyebrow at Sam, waiting for a response, rubbing his fingers against his thumb on one hand to make sure that cash was in Sam's mind.

'I can't do it,' Sam said after a long pause.

David Morgan OBE stared at him, dumbfounded. His brain couldn't quite compute what he had just heard, so he just stood there, gawping until he could regain some composure.

Jane stared at him also, in his bruised and battered state yet looking so defiant. She had thought that he would go for David Morgan OBE's offer. It was a lot of money and Sam had always talked about how great a journalist he could be if only he were given the chance. He had never been the sort of person who would make a stand for what was right. But now, as he seemed to show some principles, Sam had never turned Jane on so much. She could barely wait for David Morgan OBE to be gone so she could take Sam where he stood, or fell.

'Alright, an extra twenty K,' David Morgan OBE said, finally breaking the silence.

Sam thought about it again. Obviously, that was a lot of money, but he just couldn't work for that man. He shook his head painfully and laughed. He'd never felt wanted like this before. 'I work for Tony Maloney. P. I.'

David Morgan OBE couldn't believe what he was hearing. It was his turn to laugh again, an angry, bitter laugh. The sort of laugh forced between clenched teeth that just screamed hate. 'What?' David Morgan OBE yelled, throwing his keys at Sam for want of something better to throw at him. No one turned down an offer of a job from him, everyone wanted to work for him. 'You fuck,' he cried, 'you stupid fucking fuck. You don't have a job with Tony Maloney anymore. I had him killed.'

Sam stared at him in disbelief. Tony couldn't be killed. Not by mortal hands at least, the man seemed practically indestructible. 'Tony's dead?' Sam stuttered, tears forming in the corner of his eyes.

'What did you think was going to happen?" David Morgan OBE said, staring at Sam hatefully. And there, while looking at what stood whimpering in front of him, what he had previously wanted on his team, he came to a snap decision. 'I've come to a snap decision,' David Morgan OBE said, snapping his fingers, because he was a cunt. 'I'm afraid I'm going to have to have you killed as well.' He wished that he had some brandy and a fire for dramatic effect, but he didn't. 'And you,' David Morgan OBE bellowed, turning to Jane and pointing at her sharply with his piggy little hand and evil piggy eyes which seemed to glow red, even though they weren't. 'I'm afraid that I'm going to have to have you killed too.'

Jane would have been not only offended, but shitting herself with fear if it wasn't for the fact that she knew something that David Morgan OBE didn't.

'Yes… there's nothing else for it,' David Morgan OBE said, almost to himself, as if he were just thinking aloud. 'I'm going to have to have the pair of you killed, you've really left me no other option.' He turned back to Sam and glowered at him. 'I came here to offer you a job, I'd already made my peace with Vince and thought that you might like to come on board, but sadly, no. It's your own fault you know.'

David Morgan OBE reached behind his jacket and pulled out an elaborately decorated tanto which he threw to the floor beside Sam's feet. 'I'm going to leave now,' he said, starting to walk away, 'but some people I've retained will be with you soon. I hope that you both do the honourable thing and commit hara-kiri before they get here,' he said hopefully, heading to the door, still fuming at his offer being turned down although feeling slightly better with the thought that soon they would be dead.

But David Morgan OBE didn't make it to the door, Jane moved in to intercept him, blocking his path with her little frame. 'You aren't going to have either of us killed, you weird little prick,' she said, striking him across the face, drawing yet more blood.

David Morgan OBE stepped back in shock, he just couldn't believe that this had happened again, to him, David Morgan OBE. It was wrong, that was the only way of describing it. He had never been spoken to or treated like this in his entire life, it beggared belief. He went to punch Jane in the face, putting his whole weight behind it, but this time Jane was ready for it, dodging his clammy little mitts effortlessly, slapping him again in the face, not even hard, just lightly to annoy him. 'You're not going to have us killed,' Jane said, 'you're not going to do anything to us, you can't even touch us.'

'And why would that be?' David Morgan OBE asked, flapping his arms around wildly, still attempting to hit her.

'Because of this,' Jane said, ripping a small microphone and battery pack from about her person and waving it in David Morgan OBE's face, who just stood looking stunned, trying to work out what the fuck was happening now. 'And that,' Jane said, pointing up at all the cameras positioned around the room. She slapped David Morgan OBE around the face with the battery pack a couple of times, giggling victoriously. 'And because of him,' she said, pointing towards a cupboard, expecting to see her cameraman leap out looking especially pleased with himself, until she remembered that it was his day off.

David Morgan was still staring at the microphone, a vague flicker of recognition snowballing into a gut wrenching, shit bursting sense of panic. 'What is this supposed to mean?' he said, batting the nasty thing out of her hands. 'Is this supposed to stop me from killing you?' he mocked, making a dreadful attempt at bluffing. 'You haven't got a goddamned thing on me.'

'Apart from you on tape admitting to having someone killed and then threatening to have the same done to us,' Jane chuckled, bending over to pick up the mic, making sure she showed her ass off to the cameras.

David Morgan OBE couldn't take it anymore, things just kept getting worse and worse. He'd never been treated like this before, he didn't think that anyone had been treated like this before. It wasn't human, it was like the whole world was conspiring against him, and for no reason he could think of. 'What's to stop me having you both killed and just taking the tapes?' he growled.

Sam, who had been wondering the same thing, looked to Jane for the answer, hoping that she had a good one.

Jane looked at them both and laughed. 'Because it's stored on my computer and with the press of a button, I could have it sent to a thousand other people.'

'So supposing I just smash your shitty little computer up,' David Morgan OBE said, searching around the room with his beady eyes for the thing.

'It wouldn't make a difference. It will already have been sent to my web designer automatically.'

David Morgan OBE stared dumbly at Jane, he couldn't think anymore. He was tired. Tired of arguing, tired of trying to work out how to deal with these people. But most of all, he was tired of being undermined. He probably could have found some way of having them both killed and still managing to get his hands on that confession, but sometimes, circumstances just beat you down and you just had to play along with things, find the path of least resistance. 'Okay,' David Morgan OBE said begrudgingly. 'What is it that you want?' thinking that he was just going to have to sign a very large cheque, because at the end of the day, that's what everyone wanted, that's why anyone ever does anything, so that they can get a big fat cheque at the end of it.

Jane hadn't been thinking that far ahead, she wasn't thinking about money, she just didn't want to be killed. This wasn't her fight, it was Sam's, so she looked to him expectantly, hoping that he would step in now that she had laid the foundations for negotiation, blackmail or extortion, whatever you wanted to call it. Sam in turn, was looking at Jane, wondering what the hell it was she was trying to tell him.

David Morgan OBE was sweating profusely, darting his head between the two of them like a worried animal, a meerkat, or maybe even an owl, trying to work out in his head how much this was going to cost. He figured that it was going to be a lot, considering how much Sam had already turned down.

Jane nodded at Sam, willing him to name a price and after a few more expectant nods, Sam finally got the message that she wanted him to take the lead.

'Well?' David Morgan OBE snapped, starting to consider the murder option to be quite appealing and a hell of lot easier once more. 'Spit it out.'

'Nothing,' Sam said finally, smiling about as much as his deformed face could smile, almost laughing manically but not physically able to, making more of a dry chuckling sound, but deep down, inside, he was laughing manically, because it was fucking hilarious. All that pain and suffering and death and upset and backstabbing had come down to this, David Morgan OBE asking what he wanted and what he wanted was nothing. 'I don't want anything from you, I just want to be left alone. I just want you to promise to leave me alone, to leave us all alone and never bother any of us again. We won't get in your way and you don't get in ours.'

David Morgan OBE couldn't bring himself to believe it, it was unbelievable, which was probably the main reason why David Morgan OBE couldn't believe it. 'You're serious?'

'Deadly serious.'

It didn't seem likely to David Morgan OBE, but it was an offer worth a quick gamble on; cheaper than paying him off, less hassle than having them killed. Then he thought with a dirty little supercilious smile that maybe he had frightened the poor bastards more than he had expected. They just wanted out no matter what they had over him, happy if they managed to get away with their lives. 'You'd better be,' he said coldly, 'because deadly is what it will be if I start getting demands and threats a few months down the line.' David Morgan OBE couldn't help thinking to himself, what a prick. People just didn't turn down offers for an arse load of cash and opt for nothing instead, it didn't make any sense, but then, nothing about this strange episode made sense to him.

'It's a deal then,' David Morgan OBE said, not even considering shaking his hand, still vainly trying to pretend that he was the one with all the leverage. 'But the next time our paths cross, I can assure you that I won't be so forgiving.' He turned his back on Sam, paused for a moment and then began to leave. He went to shove Jane over as he walked past but hesitated, his hands hovering near her shoulders before he simply seemed to give up, losing interest. He plodded off, stomping out of the door feeling very sorry for himself. This had been one of the worst days of his life. The only thing that gave him any solace, kept him going, was the fact that it was all over, it was finally finished and everything would fall back into place, possibly ending up even better than before. That deal with Vincent Lee would see circulation rise ever higher, and then there was all that hara-kiri he was going to make the plebs in his office commit as soon as he got back. He jumped into his 4x4 and told the driver to drive, which he did. Fast.

'I thought you said that you weren't filming us,' Sam huffed at Jane, somehow missing the point that she had just saved their lives.

'I wasn't,' she said smugly, stepping over to Sam and helping him back on to the couch. 'I hadn't switched everything on to record yet.'

Sam didn't know what to say. They had escaped death by very little and it was the one time that she really hadn't been filming him. He thought about yelling at her but he couldn't do it. He just wanted to go back to sleep, for a year.

'I might have gotten some sound recording though,' Jane said massaging her head into Sam's thigh kind of lovingly. 'Now that we're not in any immediate danger anymore, why don't we celebrate after all this excitement with a nice bit of anal?'

Chapter Twenty

Sam stood outside of the hospital entrance, finishing his cigarette and what was left of his can of wicked strength lager. He didn't want to go in. He was scared by what he might find, scared to see someone he had once thought was so strong looking so broken.

Several people, coming and going from the hospital, stopped to stare at him, wondering which ward he had escaped from, serious trauma most likely.

Sam stumbled up to the front desk hoping to find out which floor Johnny Cheung was on. The triage nurse stared at him, wide eyed, open mouthed. 'Are you okay?' she stuttered, which was a pretty stupid question for a triage nurse.

'I'm looking for a patient,' Sam said to the desk clerk, ignoring the nurse's horror. 'Johnny Cheung. P.I. He was admitted yesterday, I think.'

The desk clerk looked at his system and gave him Johnny Cheung's details while the triage nurse was busy taking Sam's pulse and trying to subtly flick antiseptic into his face. 'I think you ought to sit down,' the nurse told him, dragging him over to an empty, piss stained wheelchair.

Sam shook himself free and dribbled away to the lifts.

'At least let me give you something for the pain,' the nurse yelled after him, brandishing a large suppository.

He fell into the oversized hospital lift, nearly landing on the floor, kind of wishing that he had at least asked for some crutches. A young doctor already in the lift stared at him, her stethoscope draped around her neck.

'You shouldn't be out of bed,' she said, wondering how she was going to coax him back onto his ward, 'not in your condition.' She paused to throw some tablets at him, seemingly oblivious to the fact they were bouncing off his closed mouth. 'Who's your attending?' she asked, fumbling to jab some sort of needle into him.

'Get away from me,' Sam cried, shoving her over, giving a sigh of relief as the lift came to a slow halt, the doors opening in their own sweet ass time. He stumbled out, a half-compressed needle still stuck firmly in his neck, and staggered down the corridor, throwing the needle to the ground as he went.

Johnny Cheung was lying in his crude, a-frame of a hospital bed, half asleep, half drugged. Sam struggled on over and dumped himself down on the crappy little visitor's chair, one of those horrid orange plastic ones like you used to get at school. He looked at Johnny Cheung and wondered whether it would be acceptable to try and wake him up, shake him or prod him a bit or something.

'It's you!' Johnny Cheung said as he began to recognise his visitor.

Sam produced some sorry looking grapes, waving them about in Johnny Cheung's face, like he was trying to prove he was a genuine visitor. 'I brought you this as well,' Sam said, handing Johnny Cheung his Gameboy. Johnny Cheung held it in his hands with glee and then placed it neatly on his bedside table.

'I thought you were probably dead,' Johnny Cheung said slowly, the painkillers the nurses had been constantly injecting him with playing havoc with his normal quick thinking. He managed a slight grin for Sam.

'Good morning,' a young doctor appearing from nowhere, managing to make the simplest of greetings sound patronising. He leaned over Johnny Cheung flashed a little torch in his eyes. 'And how are we feeling today?' he asked. The doctor had already turned his attention away before Johnny Cheung could respond and was now gawping at Sam, trying to mask a look of utter horror, just like he was taught at medical school. 'Good God man,' he cried, 'what on earth are you doing out of bed?'

Sam stared at him, bewildered as the doctor began injecting various tonics into his arm and neck.

'I don't see you getting back into bed,' the doctor told him, tapping his foot.

'I'm not even a patient here,' Sam said, his protests falling on deaf ears.

'Am I going to have to call for the Ward Nurse, she's been dying to try out her new chemical cosh.'

Sam got up, feeling it would be the easiest thing to do, and looked around for an empty bed, but there wasn't one. He thought about pointing this out to the doctor until he noticed the fool waving a larger, longer needle around in a threatening sort of a way. Sam slowly inched towards Johnny Cheung's cot, the doctor nodding in encouragement. Sam hesitated for a few moments, wondering what was wrong with the man. The doctor sensed disobedience and lunged at Sam wildly, jabbing and prodding at him with the syringe.

Sam got the message. He threw one leg under Johnny Cheung's blanket. The doctor seemed appeased by this a little and stopped the attack, but he was still poised, like a coiled spring, ready to strike again if need be.

Sam sighed and climbed the rest of the way into the bed, Sam and Johnny Cheung both swapping glances.

'Excellent,' the doctor said, sounding very pleased with himself, seeming to forget about Sam as he began to flick through Johnny Cheung's notes. 'Well, Mr. Cheung, your scans came back clear, but we still want to keep you in another night just to be on the safe side. Don't want your brain to start haemorrhaging all over the place, turning you into a useless vegetable with no one around to pick up the pieces.' He winked at a female nurse over the other end of the ward and then injected something into Johnny Cheung's drip before moving on to patronise his next patient.

'You look pretty messed up,' Sam said to Johnny Cheung, wondering if it was safe for him to get out of bed yet.

'I've had worse.'

'I'm sorry about Tony,' Sam said, looking at Johnny Cheung with what he hoped was a warm, comforting expression.

'Thanks,' Johnny Cheung said, beginning to cry but carrying on like he wasn't, not that he was embarrassed about it, he just didn't like making a big deal of things.

Sam felt like crying too but he tried not to, not that he was embarrassed about it either, he just thought that it would be disrespectful considering he hadn't even known Tony that long. 'What are you going to do now?'

Johnny Cheung thought about it for a while. 'Well, Tony left me his share of the firm, so I guess when I get out of here, I just get started on the next case. We had plenty of work lined up before all this happened.'

That wasn't what Sam was expecting. Johnny Cheung seemed too calm, although maybe that was down to his medication, but if Sam's best friend, if Sea-mouse, or Ford even, had just been murdered, his blood would be boiling. He would be out to get whoever was responsible. 'What about David Morgan?' he asked, 'What about revenge?'

Johnny Cheung stared at him, shaking his head. He had been thinking about that a lot, between slipping in and out of consciousness. Revenge didn't get you anywhere though, Johnny Cheung knew that from experience, it just left you empty.

'Not worth it,' Johnny Cheung said, 'so long as he leaves me alone, I'll leave them alone.'

'Really?'

'Vince is no longer carrying on with the case, so what is the point?'

'But Tony is dead, don't you want to get him back for that?'

'That's not what Tony would have wanted, unless I was being paid to do it. He would have been glad to go the way he did anyway, in battle, in the middle of a case.'

'What about the police?' Sam asked, slightly puzzled at how rationally Johnny Cheung was acting.

'The police already spoke to me. Those two guys we left dead in the office were known criminals, I told them me and Tony caught them trying to rob us, we had to kill them in self-defence. They even spoke about some sort of reward.'

'But David Morgan is a cunt,' Sam cried.

'You don't think I don't know that,' Johnny Cheung said, his eyes glazing over as he hit the button to pump another shot of dope into his system. 'But it's over now, it's over.'

Sam couldn't hold back any longer, tears began to flood down his face. 'He killed Tony,' Sam whimpered, 'he killed Tony.'

'I know he did,' Johnny Cheung said sounding diamorphine calm, yet he too was crying again. 'I know he killed Tony, but we've got to move on, as much as it hurts, otherwise it will consume us and there will be nothing left but hate and that's not living and that's not what Tony would have wanted.'

Sam tried to bring himself together, act strong like Johnny Cheung. He blew his nose on an old tissue he found in his pocket. 'Is there anything I can do for you?' Sam asked, trying to change the subject, 'is there anything you need?'

'Actually, there was one thing,' Johnny Cheung said after a while. 'I'm going to need a new partner.' Johnny Cheung began groping around under his bed for something, eventually managing to grab hold of a glossy white box with some sort of Royal emblem embossed on it. 'Here,' he said, chucking it onto Sam's lap. 'I got one of the nurses to go out and buy you that.'

Sam smiled awkwardly and ripped open the box and there, inside, was the most beautiful felt fedora.

Sam put the hat on, trying his hardest not to cry again. 'Do I get my name on the sign?'

Johnny Cheung's whole expression changed, making him looking even more melancholy. 'The sign stays the same,' he said, sniffing snot back up into his nose.

Sam nodded.

The diamorphine began to hit Johnny Cheung's nervous system and he started to drift off again. 'We start back at work next week,' he managed to say before passing out into doped up sleep again.

Sam waited for the doctor to leave the ward, high fiving a semi-conscious patient with gallstones on his way out.

Sam checked again to make sure the coast was clear, that there were no stray nurses about, before slipping out of the bed, crawling along the floor towards the lift like he'd seen commandos do in movies.

Chapter Twenty-One

Sam sucked at his beer through a straw. He had found it was the least painful way to drink, until he could get around to having his broken teeth fixed. Sea-mouse was staring at him again, a look of bemused wonder on his face.

'Would you stop gawping at me like that,' Sam said. 'You've been doing it all afternoon.'

'I can't help it, I've never seen you so messed up. Do you really think you should be down the pub in this state?'

Sam ignored him and carried on sucking at his beer, hoping that the double vision and feeling of nausea was due to the alcohol and not all the head trauma.

Sea-mouse necked the last of his beer, and his twelve shots of peach schnapps, and two Campari's. 'Do you want another drink?' he asked, downing the rest of Sam's pint, wandering off to get another round before Sam could even nod his head.

As Sea-mouse was stalking back, carefully clutching a tray stacked full of god-knows what, Ford sloped in looking a terrible state. He was sporting a black eye and two days of stubble, and he smelt as badly as he looked. 'Two bloody nights in jail,' he yelled at Sam, making a particular point of eyeballing Sea-mouse disapprovingly as well. 'Two bloody nights and neither one of you bastards even tried to get me out. Two stinking nights in a stinking cell, staring at dirty vomit-stained walls and you didn't even care. No one even phoned to see if I was alright, which I wasn't.'

Sea-mouse stared at Ford rather confused before handing him a coconut full of something noxious, a little umbrella and big curly straw sticking out the top. Ford dumped himself down on a chair and then grabbed the drink. He hoped some booze would calm him down a little, it seemed to work for the other two. He broke off from the drink and coughed uncontrollably, beginning to feel slightly dizzy from the fumes. He looked at the state Sam was in and quickly realised that he wasn't the only one who had been having a hard time of it, although he decided that he wasn't going to let that take the wind out of his sails. 'Two bloody nights,' he said again. 'They beat me you know? And one of them even threatened to put things inside of me.'

Sam shuddered in disgust at the thought of it. He felt guilty for getting Ford involved in all of this.

'They didn't even charge me with anything. They couldn't. I hadn't done anything,' Ford continued. He glowered at Sam, laying the blame on him without having to say it. 'I would have been in real trouble at work if I hadn't been able to phone them from the station, the police gave me that much, but it cost me…' He paused to take some more of the drink and then paused again to cough. 'I had to lie, I had to say I was in a car crash. I said I had been rushed to hospital. God, I hope no one tried to visit me in hospital, I'm buggered if they did, I'll be up on disciplinary proceedings.'

Sea-mouse looked at Sam with his eyebrow raised, but he remained silent. Saying something would have been kicking the poor bastard when he was down.

'They only released me today because they needed the cells, and they said because I didn't put up enough of a fight, it was like punching wet clay they said.'

'I'm sorry,' Sam said to Ford quietly, feeling even more rotten for putting everyone through all this shit. Like a putrid, puss filled anal fissure. He handed Ford another drink from the tray and necked some sort of shot himself, much to the annoyance of Sea-mouse who had his eye on that particular glass of gut rot.

Sam began to cry, thinking about what everyone he knew had been put through on account of him. Of course he had thought about blaming Vince, and David Morgan OBE, and Sexfiend. At the end of the day, Tony Maloney and his detectives were only pawns in a shitty game of meaningless revenge. But then, that was their choice, to be used that way. It was not as if they were inanimate objects. They were people with free will and all with a conscience. At any point, Sam could have walked away. He could have left, taken another job, any shitty minimum wage job in a call-centre or flipping burgers.

'There there,' Sea-mouse said, patting Sam's back, trying to comfort him while sneaking the majority of the drinks he had bought over to his side of the table, although not before Ford had managed to grab another.

'What are you going to do now?' Ford asked, starting to slur his speech.

'I don't know,' Sam said, grabbing a pint from the tray Sea-mouse had just hurried off to get, making sure to bring a whole pitcher back for himself, not to mention the turpentine the barman had found for him from somewhere.

'I need some time to think. I think I'm going to go home,' Sam said, practically falling backwards out of his chair as he attempted to get up.

They stumbled out of the place, except Sea-mouse of course, and the cold night air washed over their drunken skin, barely even raising a shiver through the warm, protective layer of alcohol in their systems.

'I could do with another drink,' Ford said, having another flashing thought about how empty he felt, hoping that if he drank enough tonight, everything would reset and go back to normal. Tomorrow, he could go back to being the same high-flying, high aspiring go-getter he used to be, which probably would be the case. Ford was never the sort of person to let a few uncertainties get in the way of his ambition, and with every drink he took, he was worrying less and less about all the trouble he could be in at work.

Sam still felt weak, he felt like now might be a good time to go home and sleep, but then again, some alcohol might do him some good. It was nothing but pure energy; carbohydrates and OH groups. Then there was the fact that he didn't really want to go home and be all by himself, at this late hour. He was scared despite the deal he had made with David Morgan OBE. He didn't fancy the prospect of trying to sleep in his cold, empty flat, listening out for every creak of the masonry and every rattle as the wind blew against his windows, imagining people hiding in his wardrobe and crawling through his loft, and once they'd killed him, they'd go through his things and find all the embarrassing stuff he had stashed about the place, diaries, love letters, and porn.

'Okay, c'mon, let's go someplace and get another drink,' Sam said, starting off down the road by himself, not really sure about where he was headed, hoping at some point Sea-mouse would take over with his knowledge of late-night drinking establishments in the area. Sam stopped to light a cigarette, turning to block his lighter from the wind. He so happened to glance down an adjacent road and just so happened to witness, at that very moment, by some unpleasant coincidence, what looked like a man step out and be ploughed down by a bus. He did a double take and sure enough, he hadn't imagined it. The bus stopped, reversed a little way and then stopped again. The door swung open with a whoosh and fizzing of gas. The driver got out in a panic, yelling and screaming. He looked underneath, where the body should have been and came up puzzled. He squatted down and checked under the bus more carefully, coming back up again looking even more worried. 'Holy crap, holy crap, holy crap,' he yelled, wondering where all the mess had gone.

Sam thought as hard as he could in his drunken state and seemed to recognise that man, standing there, waiting to be run down.

'You all saw that!' the driver yelled at the old codgers, climbing back into his cab. 'The fucker just disappeared.' He slammed his foot on the accelerator while the door was still closing, leaving nothing but skid marks and a bloodstained wallet behind.

Sam froze stone dead, like a statue, a really rubbish, pointless statue. He turned to Ford and Sea-mouse looking like he'd just made some fantastic discovery. 'Clive had it right. He knew exactly what he was doing all this time.'

Sea-mouse just looked at him blankly, wondering what the hell Sam was on about. He wasn't sure that his father had had many ideas over the years, and those that he did have, Sea-mouse felt fairly certain that they couldn't be considered right, not by any sane person's standards.

'Clive had the right idea,' Sam said again manically. 'The only way to make this pointless existence worthwhile is to live forever.'

'What?' Ford and Sea-mouse said together.

'The only way to make this dirty horrible existence mean anything is to live forever, to be remembered beyond your years. And the only way to do that is by doing great things, or incredibly bad things, or by taking the easier option of mystery like Clive. And there is no way I'm going to be able to do something great with my life and I don't have the stomach to do anything particularly bad, so don't you see, I've got to follow Clive. Live the way Clive lived, always looking for death.'

'What the fuck are you talking about,' Ford cried, worried about his friend's sanity, even more so than normal.

'A bus,' Sam yelled, 'I need a motherfucking bus.' He began searching around, stalking about the street drunkenly. Sam spun round, thinking that he had seen the flash of large headlights zip by up ahead. He plodded off up the street, stomping like a toddler learning how to run, tripping and stumbling yet somehow miraculously managing to stay on his feet, performing a fairly accurate impression of a crazy person as he sped to his destiny, unsure of what exactly he was going to do if he managed to find a bus and what he exactly he was going to do after.

'What does he want with a bus?' Ford asked Sea-mouse as they both stared blankly at each other.

Sam didn't make it far though, he got about twelve yards down the road before his weakened legs gave out, the unstable momentum he'd managed to build up causing him to almost fly through the air headfirst into a bush; although calling it a bush was overselling it just a little. It was more a collection of dirty dead branches used as a storage point for dog's mess, old pornography and spent prophylactics.

Sea-mouse and Ford stood over Sam looking down, scrunching their faces up at the site of the turd, dog, or possibly human, which was smeared all over Sam's trousers.

Sea-mouse managed to pull Sam up, get him back on his feet and dust him off. He produced three cans of beer from somewhere about his person and passed them around. 'C'mon,' he said, cracking his can open. 'That's no way to live. That's no way to live at all.'

About

Arthur Stanton is a complete square. He grew up and lives in the UK in a town notable only for making shoes. He has worked a whole host of shitty jobs over the years and used to drink to forget. Through no fault of his own, he is now in middle-management hell where he spends his days sitting in endless meetings, drawing pictures of pigeons and wondering what's for lunch.

More from UPP